Praise for Marie Calloway

"'Adrien Brody' is riveting, fresh, and written with a distinctive new voice."
Stephen Elliott (*The Adderall Diaries*)

"When I read Marie Calloway I feel a unique, private sense of empathy. Marie talks and responses echo in her head. She looks at her body in mirrors. Marie sees her reflection in the reactions of people around her. Reading her work makes me feel like I'm alongside her in her mind, navigating the house of mirrors of her inner life, and in doing so, I become one. I don't think I've ever read anything that's made me feel like that."
Megan Boyle (*Selected Unpublished Blog Posts of a Mexican Panda Express Employee*)

"These new works by Marie Calloway seem singularly her, and rapidly feedbacking at themselves in a way that wakes something else up, which is refreshing."
Blake Butler (*There Is No Year, Nothing*)

"[Women like Marie Calloway] pose a threat to the social order, which relies on women's embarrassment to keep them either silent or writing in socially accepted modes."
Emily Gould (*Emily Magazine*)

what purpose

did i serve

in your life

Tyrant Books
676A 9th Ave. #153
New York, New York 10036
www.nytyrant.com

"portland, oregon 2008" and "sex work experience one" were on *Thought Catalog*
"jeremy lin" and "thank you for touching me" were on *Vice*
"adrien brody" was at muumuu house

Cover and book design by Adam Robinson
Cover photos by Ryan Field

what purpose

marie

did i serve

calloway

in your life

contents

For Tom and GABM

"Because of our social circumstances, male and female are really two different cultures and their life experiences are utterly different." *Kate Millett*

portland, oregon
2008

I wondered if I should go into his apartment. Standing there I suddenly remembered something that I had once read: "We teach children not to go into stranger's houses, so why do it as an adult?" And I thought about how he seemed very nice and gentle, but remembered hearing about how rapists and murderers often came off like that. But I wanted more than anything to do this very adult thing, so I put everything out of my mind and nervously followed him in.

He apologized for the mess; he was in the middle of moving. His floor was completely covered in boxes and clothes and household things, except for a made-up mattress lying on the ground. Probably most girls would have been put off by the state of his apartment, but I thought it looked interesting and was even pleased that this room was so far off from the romantic dreamscapes girls are supposed to want to lose their virginity in.

He left me alone by the door to go use the bathroom. Not knowing what else to do, I put my purse on the ground near the door and walked over and sat on the edge of the bed.

He came over and sat next to me and we talked more, and then started to kiss. I lay down and he was sort of kneeling over me as we kissed.

"You're a lovely girl." His voice was kind of firm. I imagined he was expressing irritation with me for earlier telling him about being insecure about my looks. I felt uneasy for a moment.

I put my forearm across my forehead in order to hide my unplucked eyebrows that were visible now that he had pushed my bangs aside.

But then I reached for the top button of my blazer and struggled to unbutton the top button.

"Can I?" he asked, his hands above my blazer.

"Okay, if you can. These buttons are kind of hard…"

But he unbuttoned it quickly, with ease.

I was embarrassed that I was wearing an old plain white bra.

"…No shirt."

"No, I told you," I said, and looked up to see if he was staring at my breasts, but he was to my surprise looking at my face. I wondered if he thought they were unattractive or if maybe he didn't like breasts.

"I don't think you did tell me."

I pulled off my skirt and underwear, and then he moved his head down.

For a while I stared at the wall, and then I caught a glimpse of his head down in-between my legs. I wondered what he was doing.

After a few minutes he came up and his face was hovering over mine again.

"Did any guy ever do that to you before?!" he asked with nervous excitement. I could smell my pussy on his breath. I wondered if he was excited by the idea of being first.

"Do what?"

I had felt his face and hair rubbing against my thighs, but nothing else. (A few years later I would learn I am completely unable to feel oral sex due to past sexual trauma.)

"…Eat you out."

"Huh? Yeah, of course," I said nonchalantly, lying.

"You're like, 'well, duh,'" he said, kind of laughing, maybe embarrassed. I wondered if he was excited by the idea of being first.

He moved in to kiss me. I wanted him to kiss me, but I didn't want him to think I would want something like that, so I turned my head to the side to dodge him. But he tried again, grinning big, and we kissed and I was excited by him forcing a kiss on me and forcing me to taste myself on his tongue.

Then two of his fingers went into my vagina and it hurt tremendously. My eyes snapped shut and I started to moan both from pain and out of feeling an obligation to make him think I was enjoying it, and feeling like I wanted to excite him by moaning and groaning.

I peeked my eyes open and saw his face was right over mine, watching my reactions. He was grinning stupidly.

"God, you're wet."

He took his fingers out and held them up to the light. They were drenched. I wanted him to put his fingers in my mouth, but didn't say anything. He wiped his fingers off on my inner thighs and I pretended to be grossed out by that.

"You're like, 'Eww.'"

He started to finger me again, faster and faster and then started to roughly rub my clit and I was in so much pain I had to fight back tears. I wanted to fake an orgasm so he would stop, but I didn't know how to or what women even acted like when they came.

I kept moaning louder and louder.

"Tell me what you want," he said.

I was too shy to say anything.

He kept fingering me for a while and then stopped and got on top of me, and through his briefs rubbed his erect cock on my crotch which I liked a lot.

"Do you want this?" he asked, his voice was gentle and sweet.

"Yeah…" I moaned.

"Okay! Let me go get a thing," he said and bolted up.

I stared at his legs and ass in his green American Apparel briefs as he walked across the room. Then he was kneeling down beside me, and I could hear him unwrap a condom. I turned to look at him.

"You don't really want to watch this, do you?"

I turned my head. I wondered why he would be embarrassed to be seen doing that.

Then he said, "I think I put it on inside out…"

"Oh my God," I said and started laughing. Is this really how I'm going to lose my virginity?

"Oh my God," he mimicked.

And I felt a bit offended and wondered if I wanted to have sex with someone who had teased me.

He got on top of me and I was in pain as he tried to penetrate me. I was moaning and maybe I sounded like a hurt kitten.

He put his mouth against my ear and shushed and whispered, "Don't be nervous."

I wondered why he was saying that when I felt totally calm and relaxed. It was completely the right time for this to finally happen.

He struggled to penetrate me again, which hurt to the extent that I didn't even notice when he did finally penetrate me until I lifted my head up and saw his cock going in and out of my vagina. It was so shocking and strange and interesting looking I wanted to keep staring at his cock going in and out, but I could tell he was looking at me staring and so I felt self-conscious and lay my head back down.

Even though I had been watching pornography regularly since elementary school this was so completely different than what I thought sex would be like.

I called out his name, thinking he would like that.

"God, you're tight…" he moaned.

I wondered what that meant.

It hurt a lot. He was fucking me really hard and fast (later he would admit he was incredibly excited to be having sex with an eighteen-year-old), but somehow I loved the feeling and thought things like, "It hurts, but it hurts so good…"

He went on fucking me for a while, me lying there half out of my mind in this strange painful pleasure, moaning like a hurt kitten.

But I was suddenly overcome with shame, stemming from feeling disconnected from him and his body. I felt that this couldn't have been good for him.

"I'm sorry."

"…For what?"

There was a strong feeling of awkwardness.

I didn't know how to respond, so I just kept moaning.

He went on thrusting like nothing had happened.

But he stopped suddenly. "Do you want to like, move? Because I'm about to pass out."

What did he mean by move? Does he want me to be on top or something?

I tried to move my hips and stomach, but I was completely out of sync with him and I felt embarrassed. And somehow my movement caused his cock to fall out. We both laughed. I stopped trying to move and lay there again while he fucked me for a while longer.

Suddenly he stopped and sighed, "I feel good."

I was surprised. I didn't know it was possible for guys to just stop in the middle of sex before they came. I thought they would explode or something if they did that.

He took the condom off and held it on his fingers up to the light. I saw it was tipped with blood. I felt horrified and hoped he wouldn't notice. But he said, "Hmm…You bled a little bit."

I stared, wide eyed, internally panicking. Oh no, would he figure out that I was a virgin now? How would he react? Oh God.

But he didn't say anything more and calmly and gently got up and went to throw the condom away.

He came back and lay on the bed. It was very late, like 2 AM. I turned my body away from his and tried to move as far away from him as I could. I had this idea in my head that men hated cuddling or anything like that after sex, so I didn't want to do that and appear clingy. But he moved and pressed his body against my back and put his arms around my waist.

I slept for a while.

In the middle of the night I got up and went into his bathroom. I turned on the light in the bathroom and stared at my face in the mirror. For ten minutes I tried to see what someone could find attractive about me, but I couldn't find anything.

I went back and lay down beside him and tried to sleep.

I couldn't get back to sleep though, and started to wake him up by kissing his neck. Instantly he started to kiss me back on my mouth and then started to finger me again. I moaned loudly and this time he said right away, "Tell me what you want."

"I want you to fuck me," I moaned.

"Okay." He was smiling.

He got up to go find another condom, and after searching for a long while came back.

"I don't have anymore," he said with an exasperated laugh.

He started to finger me again.

I wanted to excite him. "I want you to fuck me," I moaned again, even though I didn't really.

"…Even though we don't have anything?" he asked, excitedly. He started to finger me faster.

I was shocked at his suggestion. I didn't know people actually had unprotected sex.

"Yeah…" I moaned.

"Are you sure?"

"Yes…" I said.

And then I was shocked. Why did I say, "Yes" when I didn't want to have unprotected sex, was terrified by years of public school brainwashing of how unprotected sex inevitably leads to teenage pregnancy and horrible diseases? Later I would realize that it was the influence of pornography on my psyche. I didn't know how to act during sex, and I had the gaps filled in by pornography, which taught me to act really horny and desperate during sex.

"Are you sure?" he asked again.

"No…" I said, shaking my head.

He stopped and we decided to go to sleep again.

In the morning we were woken up by the sound of his phone ringing.

He answered it.

"Hello?"

He listened for a minute. I heard a woman's voice on the other end.

"Sure you can come over here. I'm not doing anything. I'm just… laying here."

They talked for a bit more and then he hung up.

He said his friend was on his way over and I had to get going right away, because to be honest he didn't want his friends to start gossiping about how he was sleeping with an eighteen-year-old.

I somehow found my clothes in the disaster of his apartment and put on my bra, blazer, skirt, and underwear in his bathroom, too embarrassed to get dressed in front of him.

But I pulled up my tights in the front room and he stared at my legs with this dumbfounded look.

When I was fully dressed I went over to the door and picked up my purse.

Standing near his door, I felt awkward. I didn't know what to say.

We stood in silence for a moment.

Then suddenly he said with nervous excitement, "Can I have your number?"

I didn't know if I wanted to see him again. It didn't go with the idea I had in my head of losing my virginity to a stranger and then never seeing him again.

"Um, I lost my phone the other day…But maybe I'll find it?"

"Well, do you want mine?"

I bit my lower lip.

"You're like, 'Noo…'" he said, kind of laughing, hurt.

"No, I do," I said, feeling bad.

He picked up a piece of paper and a pencil up from off his floor and wrote his number and email and gave the paper to me, which I put into my purse.

I turned to open the door and leave, but he told me to wait.

"I get to hug you one more time before you go," he said, and wrapped his arms around my waist from behind and tenderly kissed the top of my head.

While walking home I smoked a cigarette and felt self-conscious about wearing yesterday's clothes. I felt like everyone I passed was staring at me and knew I was doing the walk of shame. A typical Portland hipster looked at me as he rode by on his bike. I turned my head to avoid his gaze.

When I got back to campus, I looked at my phone and realized I was going to be late, so I went straight to my humanities class without changing my clothes or showering.

All day long I was in pain from my vagina being incredibly sore. I wrote furiously, obsessively in my notebook all day long about what had happened. And I couldn't get the image of his penis going in and out of my vagina out of my head.

I emailed him two days later: "Let's sleep together again."

"Monday night? 10pm? CoffeeTime?"

"Okay."

When we met again in a few days my first thought upon seeing him with his gorgeous blond hair standing in front of me in his beautiful black peacoat and Burberry scarf was, "Can this person really be here to have sex with me?"

sex work

experience one

Hi I saw your ad and would love to meet you later today, I live in Blackheath in SE London, have my own place, I can pay your travel over if interested? Please get back x."

"Hi darling, sent you a message earlier, forgot to give you my mobile no: xxxxxxxxxxxxx Prepared to give you more than £200 per hour if interested? xx Btw I am an ok looking guy!"

"Ok sounds great when is a good time? We can meet at the nearest tube station to you I don't have a phone btw we'll have to coordinate over email but would love to meet asap, Emily."

"Hi Emily, thanks for getting back, I am based in Blackheath and would love to meet you about 7 tonight if that's not too late? I am not near a tube station but could meet u at Blackheath railway station or arrange taxi? Pls get back"

"I can meet you at blackheath. 7 tonight is fine"

"Ok I will meet you at the railway station at 7, how will I know you? And can you confirm that you are not part of an agency, i'm not interested in that. Sorry to ask"

"i'll be wearing the big sunglasses as in the photo and i'll have a black plaid shirt on and a black skirt w/ black tights and black heels. how can I confirm it? here's a link to my

facebook page if that makes me seem more real. will you
pay me at the station and then we'll go back to your place?
how much do you want to pay if not 200 pounds?"

"Thank you for your honesty, I will give you the £200 at the
station, then extra £100 at my place. Could I also buy you
a drink when you get to Blackheath?"

"okay it sounds fine. a drink sounds great too. thanks for
not giving me a hard time. looking forward to seeing you x"

I stared at the computer screen.

Am I really going to do this? I guess I don't have any choice; I have about 12 pounds to last me for 10 more days in London. What did I do to my debit card? The last time I remember having it was when I was buying a ticket to Portsmouth at Waterloo...How could you be so irresponsible, Marie? But I'm fixing the problem now. There's nothing else I can do, having not told any of my family or friends that I was going to England. Anyway, I want to make my own money, now that I'm 20.

*

I looked up how to get to Blackheath railway station. I felt annoyed that I couldn't just ride the tube. I had to go to London Bridge, and then take a train from there.

It was 2 PM. I got off the computer and went and tried to nap in my hostel room.

Starting at 4 I changed my clothes, brushed my teeth, straightened my hair, put perfume on, and tried to hide my huge dark circles with concealer. It was a lost cause. I figured I would just keep my sunglasses on until I was back at his place, when it would be too late for him to change his mind. I wondered if I was cheating him, by getting 300 pounds to have sex with him. I wondered why he would offer to pay more than I asked. I thought it was a bit suspicious, but I figured since we were meeting in public and he was paying me upfront it'd be okay.

*

I left the hostel at 4:30.

As I was walking to the tube station I heard whistling from across the street and turned to look. It was some Australian boys about my age from my hostel, waving at me. I ignored them.

I rode the tube to London bridge station thinking about how I had met my friend there a few days ago, and how now I was going back under such different circumstances.

On the tube there were three school girls absolutely plastered in make-up talking at length about their diets and other girls at school. They all had incredibly grating voices, even more so than most English women.

"I was good yesterday, but this morning I had toast. Oh but then for lunch I had cherries."

"Cherries are good, but the toast …"

"The other day I ate sooo much I had …"

"Did you see she dyed her hair ginger and black? Yeah, like that's attractive."

"She's *sooo* fat, it's hilarious!"

They all started giggling at length and it was so grating and I was so hung-over.

I couldn't take it and switched compartments at the next stop.

As I was getting off the train one of them said, "That girl looked really weird."

How can people like that actually exist?

I wondered what the guy would be like. I wished I had asked him to send me a picture. He had seemed like the nicest and was the most serious (I had been annoyed with and ignored the guys who asked me to send them tons of pictures and write paragraphs about "what I was into.")

I was worried I wouldn't be able to talk to him or that things would be really awkward, but I decided I'd buy beer at a convenience store and chug it before I met him, so I'd be tipsy and less nervous.

*

The train to Blackheath was annoying; I had a headache from being hung-over, and it was absolutely packed with loud Italian tourists who kept yelling and laughing almost right in my ear. I held my head in my hands. "I can't stand these fucking people," I whispered.

But then I looked at an adorable little black boy and smiled at him, I then felt slightly sad.

My train arrived at Blackheath station at about 6 pm. I walked to a convenience store and bought two Stella Artois. There wasn't really anywhere I could sit and drink it discretely, so I guzzled one can in front of a trash can, and figured I would save the other can for a bit.

A lot of people gave me looks. Blackheath was really pretty and really rich looking. Everyone was pretty and well-dressed. I felt uncomfortable.

I wondered where to wait for the guy. I decided just to lean against a wall near the exit of the train station.

Two teenagers came up to me, one a very cute girl.

"Do you get served?" she asked.

"What?"

"Do you get served?" she asked again, more slowly.

"I don't understand what you're asking me, sorry."

They walked away.

I realized she meant that she wanted me to buy her alcohol. I sighed realizing I would probably never get the chance to get a cute fifteen-year-old English girl drunk again.

I saw a kind looking business man waiting in front of the station across the sidewalk from me, smoking.

I went up to him. "Um, can I get a cigarette off of you, please?"

"What?"

"May I have a cigarette, please?"

"Um, sure," He said and gave me one.

"Thanks."

I needed to smoke because it was 6:30 now and the whole thing was starting to seem more real to me.

I tried to comfort myself with these thoughts: *I won't get hurt because it doesn't really make sense to think that will happen. Most men want to have sex with cute twenty-year-old girls. Very few are sociopath serial killers. Caroline had sex with tons of guys from craigslist and nothing bad ever happened to her. And England isn't nearly as violent...*

And then I started to think: *And anyway, I kind of don't care if I get murdered. I guess that's an immature thing to think and if something actually happened I'd be terrified, but right now, thinking about it, I don't care. I guess it'd be bad if I got murdered and then they told my parents the situation but...*

I was mostly anxious about him not finding me attractive or not showing up and me being out of money, or not having anything to say and it being really awkward.

I looked at myself in the reflective window of the train station.

"Don't worry, you look beautiful," an old man said as he walked past me.

I leaned back up against the wall, checking the clock constantly. I looked at every guy who walked towards the station, wondering if it was him. I was mad at myself again for not asking for a picture or at least a description. But I also figured it was probably for the best so I couldn't back out due to his possible unattractiveness.

Then finally at about five minutes past 7 PM, a bald middle aged man in a banker's shirt and khakis came up to me.

"Hello, it's great to see you, Emily. I was worried you wouldn't turn up!"

"Hello, nice to meet you." I said politely, and shook his hand.

"I have to go to the cash machine, but I'll be back in about five minutes okay?"

"Okay."

I wondered if he was really going to the ATM or if he thought I was unattractive and was running away.

But, no, he came back quickly.

He seemed very excited.

He led me to a pub.

"I was trying to imagine what black plaid would look like, but then I saw your sunglasses and realized that it must have been you…"

He told me about how he was a bank manager and worked for a French company and went to France all of the time. I told him about how much I liked France and wanted to go there, talked about how I liked French music and existentialism when I was in high school and François Truffaut and Jane Birkin and Anna Karina and how I had a stalker once who said I look just like Chantal Goya and how much I wanted to smoke Gauloises…I guess I didn't care about entertaining him like I was probably supposed to and was just thinking about the things I liked to keep my mind off of what was actually happening.

I told him about how I was studying art and design, how I made money designing websites and pamphlets and that sort of thing.

"You do look like an art student."

It was pleasant enough; it was like the feeling I got when I talked to my uncle whom I see at Christmas.

At the pub I told him to get me whatever cider he recommended.

I was nervous about him not having paid me right away, but I figured it was okay since we were at a pub. If he didn't pay me here, I would just leave.

He came back to our table with a cider and a beer.

"I've been like really obsessed with cider since I've came here. Like I never had it before…"

He told me the difference between lager and beer and about where he had grown up which apparently was famous for lager.

He asked me why I came to England.

Told him about how I had always liked British music and fashion especially lately I really like Alexa Chung, and how I thought that people back home would be really impressed and jealous when I told them about how I had been to London.

We talked about how much we like Marianne Faithfull. I thought about how in America you would never find a stuffy, middle aged banker who liked Marianne Faithfull.

"Do you want something else?" he asked when I had finished my cider.

"Yeah, I want a mimosa, like Buck's Fizz."

We had to mix the champagne and orange juice ourselves.

After drinking a glass I finally asked, "Um, do you want to pay me the first bit now?"

"Yeah, certainly I do," he said and reached into his wallet and handed me the money underneath the table.

I counted it quickly and put it in my bag.

It really was 200 pounds.

And now I had money, so now I was happy again.

Since I had left my parents' house I was constantly struggling with money. My first year of college I would often go two or three days in a row without eating. When I later moved to Chicago, I was sick with anxiety the first few days I lived there. Due to an error with my bank, I was going to be thrown out into the street. I got that same panicked, anxious feeling in London when I had ripped through my suitcase and purse and hadn't been able to find my debit card.

I thought then that not having to endure that kind of horrible stress and fear was worth whatever happened with this guy. *I just want lots and lots of money and expensive things so I don't ever have to be afraid of what's going to happen to me again, no matter what I have to do to get it.*

"I'm really hungry. Will you buy me something to eat?" I asked.

"Sure. Do you want a burger, maybe? The menu's right there."

"I think I want fish and chips."

"You're going to eat fish and chips and champagne?" He laughed.

"Yeah, what's wrong with that?"

He went to the bar to order me my fish and chips.

When he sat back down we talked more about London and other general things.

Somehow it got to me admitting, "You can probably tell I've never done anything like this before."

"Yeah. I mean the way you look and how you were so nervous when I first met you, it's nothing like agency girls. I mean I was nervous, too…"

"How many times have you done this?"

"This is the third time. The first two times were with professional girls and I had absolutely nothing to say to them. But with you, you seem intelligent. Like there's a lot going on behind you."

"I'm smart at some things I guess, but not with people or at growing up. And those are the important things…"

*

The waiter brought me my fish and chips. He was cute. I wondered if it looked to other people like I was here with my dad.

"Is it supposed to be a filet?"

"Yeah. It's very traditional fish and chips. They even gave you mushy peas."

"In America, fish and chips is usually like fish sticks, you know. I guess it wouldn't be authentic…"

After eating and finishing the rest of the champagne I said, "Do you wanna go?"

While walking back to his place some tween girls walking past us stopped and asked him if he could help them because they were lost. He looked up directions for them on his iPhone. He was very sweet to them. I thought how surreal it was for there to be a gang of kids talking politely to a man who was with a prostitute. I wished I had a cigarette.

"That was nice of you, to help those kids," I said.

*

His place was nice. I could tell he was well-off, I guess. But it also felt uncomfortably stark and lonely.

I sat down on his couch.

"Do you want to pay me the rest now?"

He gave me one hundred more pounds, which I put into my bag.

We talked some more.

He asked me if I thought there was anything wrong with what we were doing, and I said that I didn't think so.

He agreed. "We could have met at a pub. Of course you might not have gone home with me then, but…"

"I was only going to do it with one guy, and you seemed like the least creepy."

"Really? Only one?"

*

I asked him about his first time, since I always ask men about that.

He told me about losing it at 17. He told me about how he had fallen in love with the girl he lost it to, and how "those feelings never really go away," which worried me as someone who was still very much in love with the person they lost their virginity to, a year and a half ago.

We talked some more and it got around to him admitting, "Well, I'm seeing someone. But, I don't know if we're still together. She's in South America right now, studying yoga. She hasn't been in contact with me in a few months. I mean, people are adults, and can make their own decisions…"

There was some silence.

"Listen, Emily. I don't want you to do something that you really don't want to do. You don't have to have sex with me, you can take the money and go."'

I briefly considered it.

I'm not used to people being nice to me.

"No, it's okay. I don't believe in stealing or whatever."

He said he had to go into the other room for something. While he was walking away I took off my clothes and stood up.

When he came back and saw me he said, "Oh, that's beautiful. You're really beautiful, and like naturally beautiful."

"Yeah, I grew up mostly in Los Angeles, and there most of the girls were like fake blonde fake tan lots of make-up you know, which is cool I guess, but it was just never my thing…"

*

I sat down on his couch and gave him a blowjob while he was standing up in front of me. I didn't really feel disgusted or anything like I was afraid I would. It was okay.

But then he kneeled down and started to go down on me, which was really gross. I don't like it even when a really hot guy does it. I forced myself to moan like I was enjoying it.

When he stopped I stood up.

"Do you want to fuck me?"

"Of course I do." He sounded nervous. "Do you have a condom? Because I don't."

"Yeah, I have one," I said and got one from my purse.

He made some joke about how one should never look in a woman's purse.

We went into his bedroom, and he lay down on the bed.

I handed him the condom and he put it on.

"Oh, you want me to be on top, huh?"

So I did and again it was like whatever, it wasn't gross or disturbing.

He lay there and had an erection while I moved.

"Do you want to do it another way?"

"What?"

"Because I just feel kind of tired."

"Well, I've just cum, so. Good timing, I guess."

I couldn't believe my luck, with him being a two pump chump.

We both got dressed.

He said he would call a taxi for me.

He went to go use the phone. I sat on his couch.

"I've just called the taxi and it should be here in about ten minutes. Can I get you anything?"

"Can you get me like coffee, 'cause I'm really tired. Just black coffee, nothing in it. And toast with marmite on it, if you have it."

He went to go make me those things.

I smoked the cigarette I saw laying on his table.

I looked in my purse at all of the money I had now.

He brought me the coffee and Marmite-toast on a tray, but when I grabbed the coffee cup it was so hot that I yelped and dropped it all over his white couch.

"Oh god, I'm so sorry!"

"No, it's okay. I'm sorry for handing you that. I didn't realize how hot the cup was. Stains can easily be washed out, but scars are forever…"

I ate my toast standing.

He gave me 50 pounds for taxi fare.

"You know, Emily, don't make a habit out of this. You seem like there's a lot going on behind you. You don't seem like the kind of girl to do this."

"Well I just had to, since I lost my debit card. I only planned to do this once. And, you know, no girl wants to do this, but if I had to do it I'm glad it was with you."

"I understand, I mean especially in London, where you just seem to burn through money so fast…"

He wanted me to keep in contact with him; he said he wanted to show me London, "even though this is such a strange way to meet someone."

I lied and said I would email him.

He talked about how strange life is. "You never know what's going to happen from day to day. Like waking up this morning I had no idea that going on that website that I hardly ever go on these days would lead to me sleeping with a twenty-year-old later today…"

Then my taxi was here.

I kissed him on the mouth (he asked me if I minded and I said I didn't) and hugged him and we said goodbye.

I took the taxi back to Hendon Central tube station.

sex work

experience two

I *can't drink anymore of this. It's almost 4 anyway. Whatever is going to happen is going to happen at this point.*

I took a last sip of lemonade and threw it away after the beer I had been chugging in an attempt to alleviate my anxiety.

I walked away from the trash can I had been drinking next to, and went to lean against a wall in front of the tube station.

I wondered if I was buzzed or if it was just my fever.

A suburban looking woman gave me a dirty look as she passed me.

I saw a Middle Eastern looking guy with glasses and curly hair as in the photo and wondered if that was him, hoping it wasn't because he looked creepy with his messy stubble, and he was a bit fat.

But who cares what he looks like? As long as he pays me.

I had been telling myself this over and over.

Then I saw a guy coming from the opposite side of the street towards me, waving and smiling.

This is him, huh, I thought, bored. *He's not hideous I guess.*

I felt blank. I could feel instantly that he wasn't out to hurt or cheat me, but there weren't any positive emotions either, or even any relief in seeing that he wasn't going to kill me.

"Hello," he said.

"Hey there."

"What's your name?"

"I'm Emily."

He pointed in the direction we were supposed to walk and I followed him across the street.

"And you're Justin?"

"Justine, or Julie."

I wondered why he had such a feminine name.

As we walked he asked me general questions about how I liked London, about school, told me about his busy day, told me about how he was a hotel designer…

The entry to his apartment had so many stairs. I started panting immediately, due to being weak from being sick.

He mimicked me panting.

I laughed, embarrassed.

"Do you smoke or something?"

"Yeah. I guess I should stop. I'm very out of shape, obviously."

His apartment was incredible, with huge windows everywhere. He was obviously wealthy. His furniture was all beautiful. He had two huge Louis Vuitton suitcases just lying out in front of his closet, and a Leica M8 camera lying on his desk.

I complimented him on his apartment. He said that he had designed it himself.

"Feel free to sit down," he said motioning to his couch.

So I did and I took off my sunglasses, hoping he wouldn't think I was ugly underneath them.

"Do you want a beer or something?"

"Yeah, a beer might be nice."

He gave me some Thai beer that would have been nice if I wasn't completely sick of alcohol after my previous week of binge drinking brought on by the excitement of being legally old enough to buy alcohol in England.

He gave me a cigarette that was very harsh on my sore throat.

We talked a bit more.

And then to my surprise he said, "Let's get this out of the way."

He reached into his wallet and gave me 200 pounds.

I counted it and put it in my bag. I was a bit disappointed it wasn't the 220 pounds he had implied he would give me in his emails, but I was too shy to say anything.

"I'm sorry, am I taking too long or something?"

"No, don't worry about it. I want you to relax."

He set music on.

I realized it was Lady Gaga and I started to laugh.

I think I offended him.

I took off my shoes, and he perked up, but then settled back after he saw I went back to drinking.

I wasn't paying attention and the cigarette butt burned me and I dropped my cigarette on his table.

"Oh god, I'm sorry."

He made some funny sarcastic remark like, "Thank you for ruining my furniture," and cleaned up the smoking ash I had dropped.

I drank more and more.

I want to get this over with, I feel bored and sleepy I want to go home I want to go to sleep.

I thought about initiating sex with him, but felt too embarrassed.

"Oh fuck it. I don't fucking care," I said and stood up. Facing him but avoiding his eyes, I undid my belt and started to unbutton my dress. I could feel him staring at my breasts. I had never felt nervous like this before having sex with someone. I wondered why I was so anxious.

I unzipped my dress and took it off completely. Then off came my bra and tights and underwear.

"Where are we going to do it?" I asked.

"It's in there," he said, pointing.

I followed him into his bedroom.

I caught a glimpse of my face in his vanity mirror and thought I looked trashy and hideous.

His bedroom was also big and gorgeous.

"Your bed looks so nice!" I said, thinking how soft it must be compared to the rock hard hostel bed I had been sleeping in the past week.

"What?"

"Nevermind."

He got undressed behind some wall in his room as I lay in the bed.

He lay down on the other side of the bed.

He wasn't saying anything. I wondered what to do.

"Do you want me to give you a blowjob or something?"

"Or something?" he kind of laughed. "Yeah, that might be nice."

I thought his cock tasted and smelled sweaty, but I thought of all the sushi and margaritas I would be able to buy after this and kept going.

He was moaning a lot and seemed to be enjoying it. I could feel he was pretty hard now. I wondered if he would ask me to stop and fuck him. But he didn't say anything. I just had to keep going and going. I wondered if I would be forced to give him head for an entire hour.

I couldn't take it anymore so I finally just started to give him a hand job and looked at him.

He sat up and started to grab and suck on my breasts. I fake moaned. He started to kiss my inner thighs and began playing with my clit, with his fingers first, then his tongue. I continued to force moans, though I was thankful that at least it wasn't painful when he played with my clit like it usually is when men do.

He came up from between my legs.

"Do you have a condom?" I asked.

"Do you? Yes, of course I have a condom."

He reached for a condom on his bed stand and unwrapped it, but then indicated toward his flaccid penis.

I felt a bit offended that eating me out had been that big of a turn off for him.

I started blowing him again for a bit.

"You know what? Maybe just a hand job."

I did it kind of lazily with my left hand. I was so sleepy.

"Not so into that huh?" he said and I took my hand off and I sat up against the pillows on his bed. He began to masturbate, while staring at me. He pulled my legs further apart.

He just sat there, staring at me, while masturbating, seeming like he might cum.

He grabbed my breasts and then fingered my clit again.

Then he just went back to playing with himself.

I wondered what the hell he was doing, but I figured that if I get paid for just this it'll be pretty good.

But then I started to wonder if this was some secret plot to fuck with me without a condom or just to cum inside me somehow. I imagined myself pushing him off of me and scrambling from his bed.

"Why don't you try playing with yourself?"

I was relieved to finally be given some direction.

"Oh okay. I was like 'I don't know what's going on.'"

"What?"

I started to rub my clit slowly, again with a lot of fake, loud moaning.

I pinched my nipples with my free hand which he seemed to like.

I wondered if he would be more turned on by watching me rub my clit or fingering myself.

He seemed to like both equally.

"Ah, okay."

He got a new condom and put it on.

I was lying against the pillows and he was hovering above me.

"How do you want to do it?" I asked.

"Like this is fine," he shrugged.

While penetrating me his cock felt big and good, but then this feeling rapidly declined.

He stopped.

"I can't do it like this."

"I'm sorry."

"It's not you at all."

"Are you nervous?"

"Yeah, this is my first time paying for sex."

"Me too!" I said excitedly.

I realized that he probably hadn't been able to notice my own nervousness, being so consumed in his own.

"I thought it'd be alright if I did it with an American, but I guess not."

Did he have some American fetish?

"Why an American?"

"My girlfriend's from America. She's living in New York right now. She said that this is the only way it'd be okay."

"If it was with an American?"

"No, *if I paid for it.* She said (he put on a stern voice), 'you can't flirt with any girls at bars or club, you can't go on dates. none of that. If you need sex, you pay for it.' But I guess I need to go back to Skype sex…"

There was some silence. I didn't know what to say or do. Probably neither of us did.

"I'm sorry this didn't go the way you wanted."

"It's not you at all. If I had seen you at a pub or something I probably would have hit on you. My girlfriend wouldn't have liked that…"

He got up and got dressed so I did too.

We went out of his bedroom and stood in his living room.

"Do you want another cigarette before you go?"

"It's okay. Can you tell me how to get to the tube station?"

"It's really easy. You just turn left from my place, and then you take a right and another left, and you're there."

"Thank-you."

More silence.

"It was pretty cool meeting you, I guess," I said.

"You seem pretty cool, Emily."

We talked some more and he showed me out.

And then I was by myself again, same as before, but with money.

I started to laugh to myself.

"I can't believe I got paid for that."

I went back to my hostel and triumphantly took a nap.

the irish photographer

I wanted to know if he genuinely wanted to photograph people, or if he just said that to get girls to go over to his place. I asked Tom about it, and he said, "I think it's probably both." Tom and I had been messaging for weeks and I had been asking him about all of the guys I was interested in.

"What do you think of this guy? Very interesting. Asked to take my photo. Seems to have an Asian fetish."

"Petsheep is—well, he's honest. I wonder how much casual sex he gets off this site. I wonder how much he gets by offering to photograph girls. It feels a little bit cheap to badmouth him, though. He is from Portsmouth however, which is a big minus. If I'm not mistaken—and I may be—you aren't actually Asian. Are you Asian?"

"I'm part Korean. You can't really tell though, except I have Asian eyes. And dress Asian apparently. Anyway I think Petsheep is great. Authentic weirdo artist. I'm drawing a logo for him. Did you hear of him before?"

"I haven't encountered Petsheep previously. We probably wouldn't get along."

"Omg. 'Just so you know, have your photo as wall paper on my phone.'- Petsheep."

"Are you fucking kidding me? Petsheep sounds like one sketchy dude. Try not to get raped."

"Petsheep asked me to be his girlfriend lol."

"Fucking Petsheep. How did you answer?"

"I said 'no' and blocked him. He has pics of girls giving him head on his blog. Very weird. Why would he want a girlfriend when he has sex with like different young model girls every week? 'Your photo is my wallpaper. I want to sleep with you this evening. What I like physically must be obvious.'"

"Poor old Petsheep, the gigantic pervert. He sounds like an asshole. Maybe he was going to photograph you giving him a blowjob? Can you link me his blog please?"

I sent Tom the link.

"His blog is lame. He is lame. Lame lame lame."

"Why do think you think Petsheep and his blog are lame? He asked me what I like the best in bed."

"Petsheep is lame 'cause he is quite, quite rapey. His blog is lame because it is bad photography. His Twitter is lame because he fucking only follows you. He has a reasonably sized dick, however. Are you talking to him again?"

"How is he rapey? Seems sensitive."

"Maybe he's sensitive when you talk to him, but his external appearance is pretty psychopathic. We wouldn't get on."

"Petsheep is taking my photo Wednesday."

"Thought you'd blocked Petsheep? Are you actually going to let him snap you nude?"

"I did block him, but then I got bored and started talking to him. Then I realized I want more pictures of me, so I said he could take mine."

"Are you going to end up covered in bruises?"

"I think he's into getting beaten up, not beating girls up. Or maybe I'll end up dead, who knows?"

"Are you travelling to Portsmouth to see him?"

"Yes, I'm going to Portsmouth. Gonna see the sea. I think I won't be able to have sex with him or you either so it kind of takes the edge off."

"Portsmouth is—no joke—fuck ugly. It's one of the ugliest cities in the country. It's fucking awful."

"Do you wanna see nude photos of me?"

"I don't particularly want to see naked photos of you, as it goes. Don't take that the wrong way."

The train ride from Waterloo Station to Portsmouth is very long. There were school kids on the train dressed in cute uniforms. I wondered why they were still going to school in the middle of July. The kids gradually left the train as it got closer and closer to Fratton Station. Then outside it was fields and cows. I thought I saw Petsheep out the window, but it was the wrong station and the man was much better looking. I couldn't imagine such a good looking blond business man going to have sex with me. Two stops away, I got up and walked through the carriage to the train bathroom. I stared at my face in the mirror above the sink. "I think you'll be O.K."

The train arrived at Fratton Station at right about 5. I followed the crowd over a bridge. The station was small and empty and horrible. The blond business man was standing in the middle of the station, then he walked away. I kind of shuffled around. An old man was looking at me. I decided to stand beside a Coke machine. Then the blond business man was standing in front of me.

"You're definitely meeting me here today, right?"

His voice sounded stern. It frightened me. He towered over me. I doubled over with laughter. The whole situation was stupid. I started to worry about my face.

"I was hoping for a better reaction than that."

He laughed.

"I didn't think that I would meet you today."

We walked toward the door.

"I didn't think you would either. Do you still want to do this? You seem terrified."

He lit a cigarette.

"Can I have a cigarette?"

"Do you smoke?"

"Yeah, see."

I showed him the pack of American Spirits in my purse.

"Isn't that impressive."

"I decided to start again while I was in England."

"Do you want to try English cigarettes?"

He put a cigarette in my outstretched hand.

"Marlboros aren't English. My parents smoke these."

I told him about how I was a liar and enjoyed being that way. He asked what I had lied to him about.

"Nothing important."

"Maybe I should have lied to you about some things."

I knew he had lied about his age online. He said he was thirty, but I figured out that he was seven years older. He was an Irish immigrant. His voice was like recordings of James Joyce I listened to in high school. I complained about people in London being cold and rude.

"I could not live my life being as judgmental as you are."

I said, "I'm not judgmental."

At his place there was some guy watching TV on the other side of the room. His roommate must have been used to Petsheep bringing home random young girls all of the time. In his bedroom, four blue dress shirts were hanging from a rack.

"You wear a lot of blue," I said.

"I should start wearing another color."

"Show me your phone."

He pulled it out of his pocket.

"Why did you make that picture of me your wallpaper?"

"Why not?"

His screensaver was a slideshow of photographs, mostly porn. I called one picture "gross."

"Yeah it is, but I like gross pictures."

There were also a lot of pictures of me. He asked me if I thought that was weird. I said I was flattered. I was pretty used to guys getting obsessed with me and doing things like that. Not that he was obsessed with me. He had also downloaded music I said I liked, but I don't think he liked it.

"Do I look like my pictures?"

"Yeah."

"Do I look young?"

"Yeah. You don't look fifteen."

"Do I look fat to you?"

There were so many pictures of tiny Asian girls he had slept with on his blog.

"No, do I look fat to you?"

We talked like that for half an hour. I had been feeling nervous and now felt less so. He suddenly stood up.

"Are we going to take pictures and have sex or are we going to go to a pub or are we going to do all three?"

For some reason I hadn't thought at all about having sex with him, even though we had talked about it so much.

"I guess all three."

"Do you have ID, just so I don't get into any more trouble?"

I reached into my purse and handed him my passport.

"Passport, nice."

"The picture is really bad."

In the photo I was fifteen and chubby and broken out.

He offered me one of the cans of beer that was sitting on the windowsill.

"You have to get used to warm drinks."

"They don't put ice in the drinks here."

I began drinking.

"You know what I said?" My voice cracked a little. "I said that as long as I was young I would never have sex with someone not in their twenties."

"Have you ever had a job?"

"No."

I've never needed a job. I have a trust fund.

"Who else are you going on dates with?"

"Tomorrow I see a journalist. He's twenty-six. Then a twenty-four-year-old DJ, then a twenty-eight-year-old screenwriter, but he says he doesn't want to have sex with me."

"That's a load of shit. I think the DJ will be the best at sex."

I told him I was interested in politics, and he asked me why, and I didn't know how to answer.

"Because it affects a lot of people maybe."

"I work for a company that makes cancer drugs, and that affects a lot of people."

"I really want to have sex with you, but I think it's going to be really bloody, and I don't care, but it's going to be really gross for you. I think if I take a shower first it'll be okay."

"I think we should have sex, and then we should take a shower, and then we should have more sex."

I stared at him.

"I used to work in a lab."

I took another drink. It was my third beer and I guess I was tipsy.

"Okay! We're going to take pictures, but first we're going to take these things off."

He came toward me with a grin on his face.

I said, "I can do it."

"I'll do it."

Petsheep lifted my camisole over my head and unhooked my bra. I held my breasts in my hands. He went to his bed. I was standing there unbuttoning my skirt. Then I had to pull down my leggings and underwear, and I knew he could see my pad. I said, "Ewww." *I'm not so self-hating enough that I think my own menstrual blood is that gross, it's just embarrassing to show it to somebody. You have to act like it's gross as a kind of apology.*

"Give me a blowjob."

I got on the bed and ran my hand up and down his cock. I pushed my hair behind my ears and put it in my mouth. Right away he took a picture. I thought he would have waited until he was in deeper, but I guess it made more sense this way. I ended up on top of him.

"You should really use something." I didn't like having to say it, but it seemed like he had sex with a million people. He ignored me. "I'm not good at being on top." At that time it hurt a lot whenever I was on top. But maybe it was unfair of me to tell someone to be dominant who obviously didn't really enjoy it. I insisted he used a condom again. He got up, and I watched him put the condom on and also lube. He really didn't need the lube with all the blood. He got on top of me. I felt bad just lying there and moaning, but I didn't know how to react, he was doing it so hard. He was kissing my face and neck. He licked my ear up and down. I really liked that, so I moaned louder. He looked down between our legs and said, "Cute little pussy." His cock went soft for a moment and I thought it was my fault. I couldn't really feel anything, I think because of the blood. I lifted my legs up. He asked, "How does it feel to have sex with thirty-year-olds?" I opened my eyes and tilted my head to look into his eyes. He looked angry. *I must look very ugly right now.* I closed my eyes again. *I don't like intense emotions.* He lifted my legs up much higher. I was in pain. "Is that okay, or too rough?" "Too rough." He let go of my legs. I felt good again, so I moaned.

We looked in each others eyes. He asked, "Do you love me?" "Yeah." I moaned. What else was I supposed to do? "Put your arms around me, tell me that you love me." He sounded frantic. I did what he said, and then I said, "I want you to fuck me without a condom," and moaned. "Why do you want that?" The truth was, I was in pain because I have a latex allergy. I said, "I think it would feel good." "How's about you let me fuck your ass? Wouldn't that feel nice?" "No, I don't want to." He fucked me in silence for a while, and then asked, "Were you lying earlier, when you said you loved me?" I didn't say anything. "Were you?" I just kept moaning. It seemed like he was giving up, or at least he was moving his body slower. "Do you like it rough? Is that how all the boys fuck you?" "Yeah." "Well, you'll have to go to them then, because I like to do it slow." He turned me over and fucked me slowly. We didn't talk much after that. Once he said, "Great tits." When he got off me, I saw he was masturbating. I told him to come on my face, and he came in my mouth. I swallowed it, but I don't think he noticed. He handed me a cigarette.

He asked, "What do your parents do?"

I said, "They're like managers in casinos."

"I don't get smoking after sex. I think it's just like smoking at any other time."

I realized that this was the first time I had had sex since I was raped nine months earlier.

"Are you going to stop being so shy around me, now that I've had my cock in you?"

"No, that's not how it works. If you like me, you have to like shyness," I said.

After the cigarette, I went to take a shower.

He said, "The green toothbrush is mine."

The tub was really high up and there was nowhere to hold on while getting out, so I almost slipped on the wet floor.

I said, "This seems like a great fucking way to die."

After I got out, he went to take a shower, and I was glad to be left alone. I went on his computer and looked at all of the messages he had sent on the dating site where we met. He said he had been asking everyone if he could take their photograph, but like I suspected all of his messages were to young girls. Out of the shower he was dressed in t-shirt and jeans. His skin was all red and his hair looked darker, no longer blond, since it was wet. Somehow he seemed much older, and looked less attractive.

"Do you ever worry about like the emotional consequences of having sex with someone?" I asked. "Like lots of older guys won't have sex with young girls because they're afraid they'll get all attached."

"Do you ever worry about the emotional consequences of not having sex with someone? Like if you hadn't done it with me I'd have been heartbroken."

He was smarter than me.

"Do you always have sex without a condom?"

"No, not always."

"Aren't you afraid of getting someone pregnant or STDs?"

"What did you say earlier? 'I don't want to talk about it.'"

"O.K."

I yawned because I hadn't slept on the plane. I could tell he thought I was bored, so I made myself yawn randomly at times to be mean. Then we went to walk to see the sea.

I asked, "Remember when we met?"

"You were hiding behind a coke machine."

"What did you think when you saw me?"

"She doesn't like what she sees, so she's going to get on the next train and leave."

"When I told my friends, well not my friends but like Internet people, that I was going to meet you, they were like, 'Don't meet him! He's going to murder you!'"

"Not yet."

At the sea we sat on the rocks. I said that growing up I always thought of the Atlantic Ocean as the lame ocean, all dirty, but now that I was here it was pretty cool, and he said something about BP. I snipped his arm with my fingers, like scissors. He was wearing a large metal-link watch like grown up men wear. I asked him who was stronger, and he said definitely you. I gripped his hand and pushed, and his arm fell without resistance. Three large boats were moving on the ocean.

He said, "There's going to be a lot of ocean liner crashes today."

"Big hips sink ships, loose lips eat chips!"

I used him as a shield from the wind to light a cigarette. He took my picture and said, "You are cool."

Why would he think that? I'd been acting so uptight today. The whole time I was thinking, I don't care about impressing this person.

He said sent me a message before he went to the station that said, I think I'm not cool enough for you.

"I'm too weird to be cool."

"I'm incredibly lame."

I could see what he meant. That's why I wanted to meet him. All of the guys I had met who were at all interesting were also insecure and pretentious.

He said he had a lot of cool friends, and one who had been in all sorts of magazines. When I dated cool older guys it was always a disaster meeting their friends, even though they were usually nice to me.

"You have nice legs."

He grabbed my thigh.

"I do have nice legs."

We looked at the sea in silence.

I asked, "Can I touch it?"

"Yes, I think you are able to touch it."

We stood up and I clutched onto his wrist and elbow, one hand around each. The beach was all stone, and I was wearing pumps.

"My shoes are going to get all messed up. Oh, well, I don't care."

We ran up to the ocean, me clutching him tightly, and I leaned down and just barely put my hand in the water.

Then we walked to a convenience store. I saw a meat pie and said I wanted to try one. We don't have them in America. He said it was going to be gross, but asked, "Should I pick one out for you?" He reached over me and grabbed one. "This is the traditional one I guess." I like it when a guy makes decisions for you, buys things for you. "Do you want anything else?"

"Oh, I wanted to try biscuits." I took a package of them.

"Do you want English beer?"

"Yeah."

He paid for it. I stood near the entrance with my arms folded. On the walk back to his place, I pulled him up to a big glass window so we could see how we looked together. I stared and said, "No, we do not look cute together."

Back in his room I sat on his bed, he showed me his teddy bear and asked me if I thought it was sweet how he had a teddy bear.

"No, I don't think it's cute."

I lay down on the bed and he sat in the chair at his desk. I asked him what he was like as a kid.

"I was very quiet. I went to catholic school, but I never really grew up. I sleep with a teddy bear."

Older men always say that they never grew up. In Portland they claim to be so young and in touch but they have no idea about anything current and listen to rock music from the 90s. Petsheep was kind of different but not entirely. He poured beer into a film canister and put it on the table near his bed. He asked if he should put the pie we bought the oven.

"Okay."

He winked at me as he left the room.

I said, "That's gross."

When he came back he started to unbutton my skirt. I liked being undressed. I closed my eyes and lay down. Then I looked and saw him batting my right breast back and forth with his hands.

"What are you doing?"

"Playing with your tits."

"O.K."

"I hope you're not expecting like profound answers from me."

I was naked now, lying down. I ate a biscuit.

"Are you going to eat biscuits in bed?"

I laughed for a long time, but the biscuit was disappointing.

"These are just like cookies, but not as sweet!"

I lit a cigarette and flicked ash into the film canister.

He asked if he should get my pie out of the oven before it burnt. "It doesn't matter. It's going to taste the same."

When the pie came out, I said, "Wow, this looks really gross."

I ate just a part of the top of the crust.

"Give me a blowjob." He was sitting in his chair.

I felt embarrassed having to kneel down in front of him, but once I started I enjoyed being on my knees. He would sometimes thrust upward so that his cock went deeper into my mouth. I liked that too. I heard a clicking sound and got scared. I looked up and saw he was lighting a cigarette. I wondered if I would ever have that kind of confidence and if he was enjoying degrading me. I felt extremely turned on and zoned out for a moment. He was making these high pitched moans. I never heard a guy make sounds like that. I was glad I could make someone make those sounds, but as soon as I became too conscious of what I was doing, he stopped. I blew him for a while longer then stopped and went and lay back on the bed.

He stood up and went to his computer and tweeted, "A very nice blowjob."

I drank three beers and started yawning.

He said, "I don't want you go to sleep now and then wake up at three in the morning and say, 'Let's drink!' And then I go to work drunk." He put something in my mouth, and I closed my throat.

"What is that?"

"Grape gummy." He had a whole jar of them by the bed.

"I don't like sweet food."

We talked for a time and again he said, "Give me a blowjob. And then you can go to sleep."

I got out of the bed and crawled over to him.

"Do you like giving blowjobs on your hands and knees?"

"Yeah." I moaned. I was very turned on.

He laughed at me, and that was unfair. I had answered the question the only way I could. I started sucking his cock and again he lit a cigarette.

"Good girl." It was like I was his dog. He was humiliating me but I felt safe and warm and completely turned on. Nothing could be more enjoyable than this. To be dominated and degraded was what I wanted. Sex is just a way to get those things. I felt valued, even though I actually wasn't. It didn't matter. Someone really wanted me and I didn't have to worry about anything besides making him feel good through a blowjob or whatever it was he wanted. Then he pushed my head down. I started to have flashbacks of being raped, having my head forced down, gagging. I tried to resist but couldn't. I gagged three times. He moaned the third time I gagged. He let go of my head. I looked up at him, shaking. He looked at me and gasped. He turned his head to look for his camera, but he didn't grab it. I got up and lay down on the bed and turned towards the wall. We went to sleep.

We woke up three times that night. The first time he said, "You are so cute! What are you, if not cute?" The next time he said, "I like my fictitious American girlfriend." The last time he said, "Try to go to sleep!" He snapped. I fell asleep feeling chastised.

I woke up at around 6:30. He was still sleeping, and I was bored, so I started to kiss and bite his neck.

"I can't go to work with marks all over my neck."

I had never had a job. I turned my head away and tried to go to sleep again.

"Suck it." He pointed toward his erection. I slid down the bed and did as I was told. "Good girl." I stopped when I got bored and lay back down next to him. He told me to blow him again. When I stopped again he hovered over me. "Down." We had hard sex from behind. "Try to keep your voice down," he told me. He never came. He threw the condom down next to the bloody one from the night before.

I got dressed.

"Hm, cute ass," he said, and pinched it through my leggings. This offended me.

"Do you want coffee?"

"Yeah."

We sat across from each other. I drank the coffee and smoked. He took a picture of me with a Polaroid camera. I asked him why he sometimes used his film camera and why sometimes he used a Polaroid.

"Why do you wear certain shoes some days and different shoes others?"

"Do my breasts look big while I'm wearing clothes?"

"Yep." He showed me the developed Polaroid. I thought I looked very cool, with long dark hair and being so thin and holding a cigarette. We walked to the train station holding hands, mostly in silence. I never want to talk in the morning.

As we got near the station a crowd could see him in his suit and me looking like a schoolgirl.

At the gate to get on the train I stopped and looked in my purse for my ticket.

He asked, "What's going on?"

"I was looking for my ticket."

"You have it or you don't have it?"

"I do have it."

"Well, you have plenty of time. My train's been canceled."

I stared at him. He said before that we would ride the train together part of the way, to his stop.

I asked, "Will we have to wait for a new one?"

"I have to take the bus."

You are so dumb sometimes, Marie.

"Okay. Goodbye."

We kissed.

On the train back to London I spaced out. In Waterloo station it occurred to me that I had spent the night with a man three years younger than my dad. At my hostel I changed my clothes and brushed my teeth and straightened my hair and got ready to have sex with Tom later that day.

cybersex

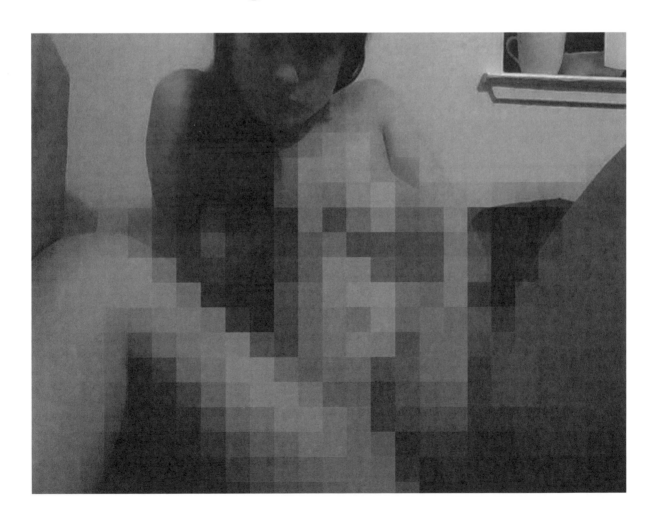

Marie Calloway
do u have rape fantasy

not really
like it sort of turns me on
but i don't fantasize about it really

Marie Calloway
k

do you

Marie Calloway
hm

?
want me to rape you?

Marie Calloway
oh

Marie Calloway
message didnt go thru

yeah shoddy internet on the bus

Marie Calloway
fantasize about someone having sex w me while im asleep or very drunk
and theyre not so i guess those are rape fantasies but not the violent
typical rape fantasy i guess i dont have

yeah i am like that too
do you want me to get you really drunk and fuck you

Marie Calloway
yes

mm yes i like
we'll go to the bar
you'll be very drunk. i'll have a bit
then i'll make you drink more at your apartment

Marie Calloway
k

hm. maybe i'll leave your clothes on
for that

lol fkjhghj im like turned on or whatever now i feel sex frustrated

Marie Calloway
k
mew
tel me weird things youre into

idk like nothing out of the ballpark rly just like pinng girls down pinning

Marie Calloway
k

holding their arm behind their back while doing them from behind and like pushing their face down

Marie Calloway
k
mew
how does it make u feel

hm
in chrage i guess
animalistic

Marie Calloway
k

raw
u know like how animals in the wild pin down their mates and its kinda a struggle
not that i wanna hurt anyone or whatever

Marie Calloway
kk

idk are u into guys doing that?

Marie Calloway
yes

hehe
lol i guess this isnt that weird either but its cool when like the girl lays down on her back and i kinda like fuck her mouth or whatever
thats cool

Marie Calloway
ya
i like that 2

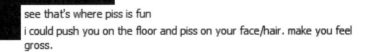

see that's where piss is fun
i could push you on the floor and piss on your face/hair. make you feel gross.

 Marie Calloway
yeah

 Marie Calloway
id like that
mew

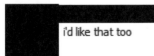

i'd like that too

ok then facefuck with cum on face, no condom issue
i guess we feel differently about doggie
thanks for reaching out, this is cool for me

On Wed, Feb 15, 2012 at 6:39 PM, ██████████████████ wrote:
Idk either is fine but my apartment has no bed only a couch etc and nothing to do here.
Just desire to have v degrading/rough sex w someone who does not respect me etc (feels fake/contrived with boyfriends etc)
Ok would be happy to be facefucked by you ending with you cumming on my face. I like doggy the most?? I also dislike condom but use them 99% of the time

Sent from my iPhone

On Feb 15, 2012, at 6:28 PM, ████████████████████████████████

i like gentle or attentive bjs from girl; or face fucking on my end -- either yanking/pulling hair from above, or her upside down head cocked back. no hand from girl, just head/mouth. hands suck, mouth is it. i've never facialed anyone, want to. also i like girls who swallow, duh. i've only ever been swallowed by prostitiute (i'm STD free, btw). i probably like bjs more than vag or ass -- it's probably a wierd need to be accepted and consumed vs. just sex

its selfish i know i'm a guy, and besides we're talking no respect. i could go down if you wanted it, of course.

with vag i'm normal, just missionary or cowgirl. doggie is boring to me, i like eye contact. love eye contact. recently did anal and it was great, much tighter. would like to try to maybe. also hate condoms, just can't, but if i have to. ive gotten rougher after last two lovers: hair pulling, neck grabbing, light choking, head holding/forcing, etc. i like sweet sex too, but since we dont' know each other that seems unlikely.

cute pic, send more pls

Marie Calloway
hm
more ppl like piss than i knew

 dudes especially

 it's a big guy thing
unfortunately
women seem to more get into it after trying it. guys are just like born
into it.

 Marie Calloway
mew
mew
what weird things have u done

 i've made someone drink my pee in a public restroom and then go back
out with their mouth full of pee

 Marie Calloway
oic

 Marie Calloway
i dont think i could do that

 do public things freak you out

 Marie Calloway
no
drinking piss

 ohh, it's not that bad actually.

 unless it gets cold
then it's horrible

pull those covers off so i can see my pretty pet
move the camera toward your waist
i wanna see your pretty pussy
lift your right leg up

rub your clit
good girl
put yr finger in
i wanna see your pussy closer to the camera baby
yeah now spread those lips for the camear

o mm
now lick your fingers and put them inside u
sexy baby
mm i would love to love your body all over
u have a beautiful luscious pussy

i can see it get wet and puffy
naughty pet

choke yourself

 Marie Calloway
talk 2 mee
;_;

 both hands
slap
harder
harder
gag yourself

Can't stop thinking about this. Woke up early thinking of it with
hard on. Couldn't go back to sleep.

▮▮▮▮▮▮▮▮▮▮▮▮▮▮▮▮▮▮▮▮

On Jan 7, 2012, at 11:52 PM, kahimikarie@yahoo.com wrote:

> Want you to cum in me
> Keep thinking abt it
>
> Sent from my iPhone
>
> ▮▮▮▮▮▮▮▮▮▮▮▮▮▮▮▮▮▮
>
>> Want right now. Marie...
>>
>> ▮▮▮▮▮▮▮▮▮▮▮▮▮▮
>>
>> On Jan 7, 2012, at 11:06 PM,
>> kahimikarie@yahoo.com wrote:
>>
>>> I'll show u naked body
>>> over skype when u want
>>> ^^
>>>
>>> Sent from my iPhone

Me too. Never been "involved" with someone younger.

▮▮▮▮▮▮▮▮▮▮▮▮▮▮▮▮▮▮

On Jan 8, 2012, at 10:26 AM, kahimikarie@yahoo.com wrote:

> Excited abt age gap/adult life gap
>
> Sent from my iPhone
>
> ▮▮▮▮▮▮▮▮▮▮▮▮▮▮▮▮▮▮▮▮
>
>> Actually don't think I would IRL. I am "all talk."
>>
>> ▮▮▮▮▮▮▮▮▮▮▮▮▮▮▮▮▮▮▮▮
>>
>> On Jan 8, 2012, at 8:37 AM, kahimikarie@yahoo.com wrote:
>>
>>> Excited by you cheating
>>>
>>> Sent from my iPhone

Fantasy of coming home from work. You are in nothing but apron and high heels. Hand me cocktail and go to your knees. Unbuckle pants and begin blow job.

After ~3 minutes I turn you around and bend you over couch. Hand you my cocktail. As I penetrate you from behind you are holding my drink outstretched trying not to spill. I'm going harder and harder and you are completely focused on not spilling my drink. Becoming more difficult as I work you harder.

I finish and you are excited to hand me drink. You haven't spilled a drop. I take you shopping for presents because you have been such a good little wifey.

On Jan 17, 2012, at 11:13 PM, Kahimi Karie <kahimikarie@yahoo.com> wrote:

the more u pull away the more i want u

but it was not meant 2 be

but sex things: i like forcing girls to do things and especially things with my cum
yeah you can

Marie Calloway
Like what

hmm. like cum on her face and smear it in with my dick and then wipe it off with her panties and put them in her mouth and so on

Marie Calloway
Sexual frustration
Want a guy to cum on my face and wipe it off with his fingers and make me suck them etc

hmm. can i fuck your mouth before doing that?

Marie Calloway
Yeah iblike mouth fucking a lot

do you gag

Marie Calloway
Yes strong gag reflex

good i like that

Marie Calloway
Want to lick a guys shoes clean sigh

Marie Calloway
f
want u to hit/piss on me
sigh

 I would definitely hit and piss on you
I'd grab your hair and throw you around, and slap you across the face
and spit on you
Then I'd get out my cock and piss all over your face
I'd make you my little toilet bitch

 k
mew
what other things do u like besides piss

 Spanking, caning etc

 But that's like, a british thing. I've never met anyone from another
country who is into that

 Marie Calloway
k
mew
y do u like those things

 I dunno

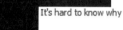 It's hard to know why

 Marie Calloway
k

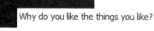 Why do you like the things you like?

Marie Calloway
K
Oh well u tell me what else u like to force girls to di

 stand on your knees and keep my balls in your mouth while i masturbate on you

 Marie Calloway
Ic

 choke yourself while i'm fucking you

 drink my cum

 Marie Calloway
yes

 gargle with it

 Marie Calloway
whatever u say

 good girl
i'm gonna cum in your panties and rub it all over your face

no you didnt yet
thank you
is that cum in your mouth

Marie Calloway
maybe

mm
you like the feeling of it hitting your face and throat
your ass is round and nice

Marie Calloway

ye you just sent that one

Marie Calloway
the video?
hmm

like, it doesn't have to be those things specifically

Marie Calloway
k

the idea of degradation in general turns me on

Marie Calloway
k
so no idea what would turn u on the most ?

hmmm
i'm not sure. i think it would be a combination of making you throw up
and pushing your face in it and hitting you and you crying while i force
you to keep sucking my cock

Marie Calloway
k

"the best part of you on your hands and knees is how easy it is to go back and forth from long deep strokes to grinding and how i can just pull out and rub the head and shaft over your clit. i like that."

"this wouldn't be the first time i've cum thinking about you. i'd be down on you right now lightly running my wet thumb over your clit while my tongue slightly runs between your lips"

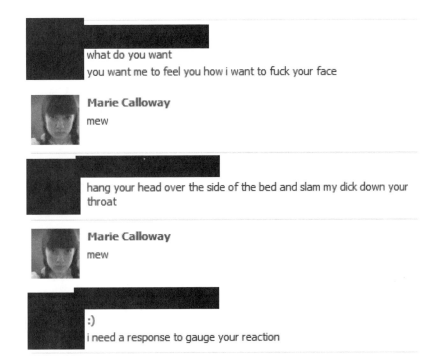

what do you want
you want me to feel you how i want to fuck your face

Marie Calloway
mew

hang your head over the side of the bed and slam my dick down your throat

Marie Calloway
mew

:)
i need a response to gauge your reaction

September 28, 2011

like she was sore from my fucking her etc
that would turn me on

Marie Calloway — September 28, 2011
really want to be used like sex doll
k

say more — September 28, 2011

Marie Calloway — September 28, 2011
like
have to lay there with legs spread and mouth open and guy uses me
however he wants

good — September 28, 2011

Marie Calloway — September 28, 2011
keepeyesopen

i'm going to use you — September 28, 2011
wear heels while being my sex doll

Marie Calloway — September 28, 2011
k

Marie Calloway
k

and lots of makeup so i can make it run

Marie Calloway
yes lots of eyeliner and stuff

yes
i'm going to hit you and call you a bitch

Marie Calloway
k

and make you rub my cum into your face

Marie Calloway
in my eyes

yeah
i'll hold your eyes open while i cum in your face

Marie Calloway
mew
y do u like cum in mouth??

 Marie Calloway
mew

 hi

 Marie Calloway
y do u like cum in mouth??

 i dunno
i don't know why i like any of the things i do in sex

 Not everyone's gonna be into it, but I like a girl calling me daddy.

 Marie Calloway
Y

 It's just naughty. Wrong. I dunno, it's submissive and hot.

 thats very feminist of you lol

sex work
experience three

I *need money for BareMinerals foundation and MAC lipstick and soy lattes and* *pizza. If I earn money I will no longer be a financial burden on my parents; I* *will be productive and accomplish something. I will be a commodity, and I will* *be in demand and valuable. I am so beautiful and young that men will pay three* *hundred dollars to have sex with me; sex work will reify my youth and beauty. I* *have no friends and nothing to do except school and this will give me something* *to do and a way to study other people besides through the Internet. I'll find out* *for myself what sex work means, and what kinds of men pay for sex and why they* *do it.*

*

I stood out in front of my apartment, waiting.

I could tell it was him the minute I saw him get out of his black SUV.

He was very tall and bald; I guessed he was in his mid-30's. He was wearing an orange hoodie and khakis.

"Are you Emily?"

"Yes."

Most clients were nervous, but he didn't hesitate before he walked ahead of me to my apartment door.

I followed him in. I shut and locked the door behind us.

We stood in the entry way.

"Do you want to get payment out of the way?" I had gotten in the habit of saying this firmly, robotically, but here my voice cracked because I was intimidated by his confidence. I was used to feeling like I had all of the power over the scared, pathetic johns, but with him I had the same feeling as when

I was a little girl and my father called me into the living room for a lecture. There was that same guilty, anxious feeling.

"Here you go."

He handed me the money. I counted it. Normally I went into the bathroom and hid the money, but now I felt too scared to do that. I just put the money on top of my dresser, which was in arm's length of where we were standing near the front door.

"Um, do you want to sit down?" I asked.

"What? I couldn't hear you. You talk too quiet."

"Do you want to sit down?" I asked again, forcing myself to talk louder, and motioned towards my couch.

He went and walked and sat down on my couch, and I walked after him and sat stiff and rigid, feeling unbearably nervous and awkward.

I faced straight ahead.

I have to say something to him but him but I can't think of anything to say.

We sat like that in silence for twenty seconds with me desperately trying to think of something to say, but my mind was completely blank.

I decided to just stand up. I stared at the blank white wall to the right of his head. I began to take off my clothes. After that extended awkward moment, I felt like I was in a race to take my clothes off as quickly as possible. I was afraid of him losing his patience with me.

You have to keep the customer satisfied, Emily, or he might take his money back.

I just stood there naked for a moment while he looked me over.

"Oh. You're cute."

"Thank-you," I muttered. I am not "cute," I am extremely beautiful. (Around normal men, I had severe anxiety about the way that I looked, but with johns there was this resentment, this bitter anger at the thought that my immense physical attractiveness could even be a question to them.)

"Can I take some pictures?" He asked.

"No…" I said weakly.

"No? I can't do that?"

I shook my head. I'm not going to give you anything extra.

He unbuttoned his pants and pulled them down. I was disgusted by the sight of his tight, dingy grey briefs.

I sat down next to him, and he stood up.

He rubbed his penis all over my face.

I get turned on whenever I watch this happen in porn, but now it's happening to me and I feel sick, though also slightly turned on. *I want to like this more.*

He touched his penis to my lips and I opened my mouth mechanically.

He placed his hands on the back of my head and gripped my hair and began to move my head wildly back and forth.

My eyes were shut tight. I stopped thinking then and was only aware of the pain in my throat and how much I wanted to gag but I couldn't. *I can't show any weakness, I can't let him humiliate me. I can't let him win.*

This continued for minutes and I felt irritated.

Why won't he just fuck me so he'll cum in a few minutes and then this will be over?

"Look at me," he said.

I opened my eyes and looked up at his face. Usually my eyes were always closed during sex work, so I could dissociate from the experience. Maybe he knows why I close my eyes and that's why he's forcing me to look at him.

"Have you ever had your mouth fucked before?"

Why is he asking me questions when my mouth is full of his penis and I can't talk?

He began to jerk my head back and forth even faster and I became very dizzy.

I finally gagged and started to cough and gasp.

"It's a lot of cock to swallow, sweetie."

It's big, but it's not that big.

He pulled his penis out of my mouth.

"Let me fuck you doggy-style."

I positioned myself so I was on all fours. I turned my head to make sure that he put a condom on, and when I saw that he had I turned my head forwards hoping he hadn't seen me looking back, and I closed my eyes.

He penetrated me and he thrust his hips so fast and his penis went so deep inside of my vagina that it caused a sharp pain. I forced myself to fake moan, like I was enjoying it, but sometimes gasps and cries of pain escaped.

"How many guys do you fuck a week? Ten? Fifteen?"

"Um, three or four…"

He wants me to degrade me; he wants me to degrade myself. What if he demands his money back at the end if I don't do what he wants?

"How many, princess?"

"Usually two a day, sometimes three…"

"Do you fuck black guys?"

"Yeah…" I could feel blood rush to my cheeks as I was so incredibly embarrassed.

"What guys your favorite?"

"Um…"

"Black guys?"

"Um…"

"White guys with big cocks?"

"Yeah…"

He laughed at me.

"Tell me how much you love my cock, you nasty slut."

I was scared and humiliated to the point where my mind was numb.

"I love your cock," I half cried from the pain.

He laughed at me, and slapped my ass really hard. I cried out in pain.

"You are a horny little thing."

I had to blink back the tears that were welling in my eyes.

(I entered, temporarily, into a bizarre mental state induced by my need to disassociate from the humiliation, the pain, and my disgust at my willingness to engage in it.)

"You like being submissive don't you?"

"Yeah…" I moaned.

I have to go along with this to get paid because I'm a whore. I deserve to be treated like this it's my job I have to make him happy. I'm getting off on being treated like this and I like it. I love it. I want to be treated as a worthless whore, I am a worthless whore. I feel so relieved. I don't have to think or impress. I'm so tired of lying to myself and keeping up the illusion that I'm not a worthless sex object when I am, I am, I so obviously am. I am a stupid worthless whore and I like being treated like one.

"I'm going to cum in your mouth."

"Okay."

"What do we say?"

Yes, I want to beg for his cum. He is going to cum in my mouth because he wants to degrade me, he sees me as less than human. He is honest and it's a relief. I am so tired of men pretending that they see me as something other than a whore, that they see any woman as anything other than that.

"…Please," I muttered.

He ejaculated in my mouth.

I love the taste of his semen.

I gagged.

I got up immediately and ran to my bathroom and spit the semen out and rinsed my mouth out.

When I came back out he was standing near the door, fully dressed.

"Well, thanks, sweetheart."

I tried to say, *no, thank-you, I hope I see you again*, but I just found myself nodding.

I walked him to the door, smiled at him, and then shut the door after he left.

I collapsed onto the floor and curled up into the fetal position and began to hyperventilate and sob.

men

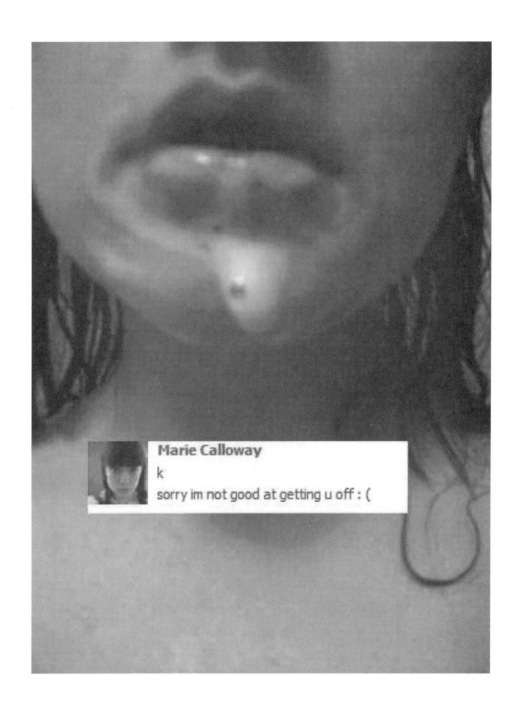

Marie Calloway

k

sorry im not good at getting u off : (

Wow! I am doing a reading with Tao Lin-what a dream come true. In school I was ostrachized because of my looks and awkwardness-but this means I am cool and attractive-wow-what a dream come true.

Do they think I'm pretty???????????

in the middle of the night i got up and went into his bathroom. i turned on the light in the bathroom and stared at my face in the mirror. for ten minutes i tried to see what someone could find attractive about me, but i couldn't find anything.

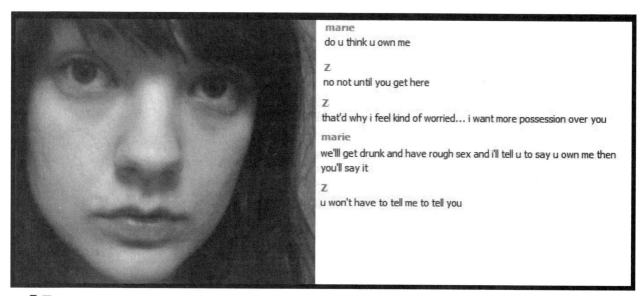

marie
do u think u own me

z
no not until you get here

z
that'd why i feel kind of worried... i want more possession over you

marie
we'll get drunk and have rough sex and i'll tell u to say u own me then you'll say it

z
u won't have to tell me to tell you

(he never did)

i like you to show me how hard people make you take it
il like the ideA of my roommate rubbing his cum on your face

Marie Calloway
he did
yay

the fucked things people made you do
yes

Marie Calloway
your roommate kind of raped me
was exciting

you didnt want him and he had you anyways

Marie Calloway
yeah
i kept saying stop and trying to push him off
but he kept going until he came in me

he was naked on skype and only got
erect when i talked about his
roommate/best friend raping me

Marie Calloway
oh
u came
cute

his roommate/best friend/my then boyfriend.
when z was gone he came out to smoke cigarettes with me.
"i like your skirt."
"do you think i need to wear leggings under it since it's so short?"
"no."

i always hoped you didnt like me

Marie Calloway

why

so i wouldnt want you

Marie Calloway

o

i thought u didnt like me

also u r asexual

so i didnt try to have sex with u

you could of had me i wanted you so badlty

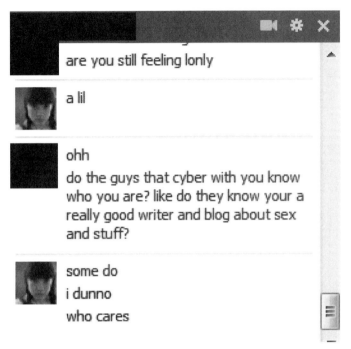

are you still feeling lonly

a lil

ohh

do the guys that cyber with you know who you are? like do they know your a really good writer and blog about sex and stuff?

some do
i dunno
who cares

[sic]

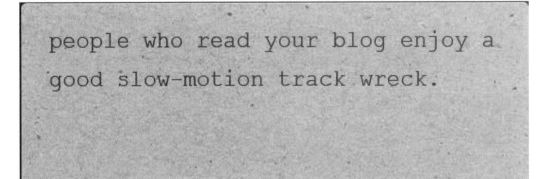

people who read your blog enjoy a good slow-motion track wreck.

Sent to mariecalloway

what is it u like abt webcam sex with me

 Marie Calloway
i like you getting off to me
i like how your penis looks it turns me on idk
i like how u touch your balls
and i like your cum idk
turned me on a lot when u came

 what about it hehe

 Marie Calloway
idk
its pretty
and hot
imagine u cumming in my mouth/face
like that i made u cum

How embarrassing!!!!!!!!!!!!!!!

Marie Calloway
i love u
want to be near u
i bought u flowers b/c i love u

Marie Calloway
i can
i mean
i dont like people to lie

you have no idea who i am
im just trying to open up to you sexaul
yoour just
you seem to know what you want
it turns me on
love might come after
my feeling are sexual

your want to get fucked my my "larger" than z   cock
lier
its cute though
can i see your face again

Marie Calloway
k

■ You called

Marie Calloway
k
idk
just want to be violently fucked all of the time
but no one wants to have sex w me

you can not accept if you feel uused

There's absolutely nothing interesting about this girl. She's half-conceited, half-insecure, moderately slutty in a dull sort of way, fancies herself to be a writer, yet lacks the talent to produce a even a decent grocery list... she's utterly boring in every way.

She's stuck between "cute" and "funny-looking", in that zone where a woman might appear exotically beautiful in one photo, yet a slight change in angle or lighting makes her look like a deranged crackwhore in the next.

She's just dull; a complete waste of time.

can i see your face again

Marie Calloway

k

You called

can i see your face again

 Marie Calloway
k

▣◀ You called ███████

can i see your face again

 Marie Calloway
k.

▣◀ You called ███████

["When men say 'I love you' they mean 'I own you'"]- Simone de Beauvoir
(he never did.)

i feel like i've learned and been told over and over again that sex won't make men fall in love with you and pretending like it will is hurting me, but i never knew a man could hurt you so much by withholding sex.

"A lot of people want to rip Marie Calloway to shreds. She is a spectacle because she has made herself vulnerable; her transparent desire for affection entertain in part because it is sad, and frightening, and such a very perfect reflection of so many people's desires. As though a desire to be told that you're worthy makes someone lesser. It does not, but in extreme cases, it may yield weird results... It comes back to Andy Warhol, a man whose profound obsession with recognition was rooted in his own profound insecurity with his appearance (and his uncertainty of his own worth or worthiness). There is always a great deal of anger directed toward those who want fame and pursue unusual means to attain it.... there is something fascinating, something profoundly intimate, about directed self-absorption...need and confusion...the fear that honesty could only be permissible in juvenilia....Marie Calloway intentionally lets the raw edge of her damaged youth show."

Marie Calloway

when im done smoking tell me to do things for u to sexually excite u

i like when u look at my dick while ur fingering urself
and i can tell it turns u on or whatever

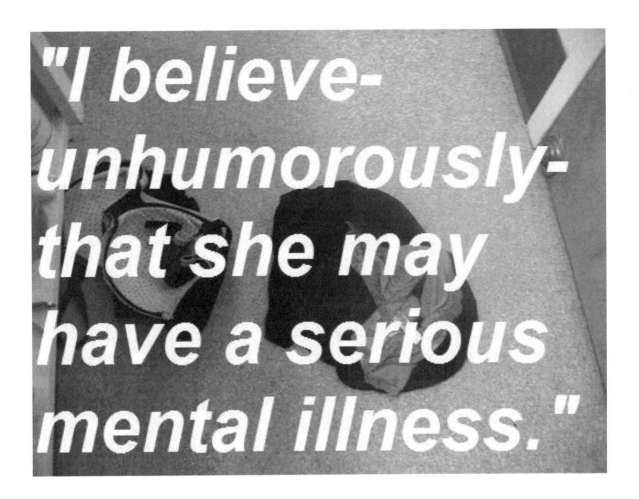

"I believe- unhumorously- that she may have a serious mental illness."

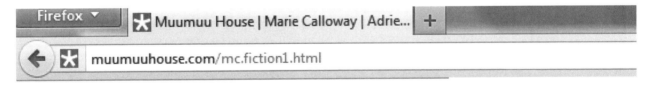

I gripped my legs tightly and kind of tilted my head to the side.

"I just used to be really insecure about my looks...like for years I felt so ugly I wanted to die."

"I can definitely relate to that."

I was surprised. I didn't know men could feel that way.

adrien brody

hello.

i'm marie calloway.

thanks for your XXXXXXXX XXXXXXX blog and other writing. especially your essay on pornography called XXXXXXXXXXX XXXXXXXX. those things have really broadened my mind. (before was strict classical marxist.)

please look at my tumblr if you want."

I sent that email in March. He didn't respond for months, so I felt a little embarrassed thinking he must have seen my email and ignored it.

But then I got this response in May:

"thanks for reading!

You can tell I don't check this email account very often, too lazy even to set up a forward — sorry for not responding sooner — I will start following you on tumblr —"

"thanks for replying

I didn't know you have a tumblr

I couldn't find a non XXXXXXX XXXXXX XXXXXXXXX email for you.

if you want please read my writing zzz

http://thoughtcatalog.com/author/marie-calloway/

tao lin liked both stories zzz

x"

"I liked the Thought Catalog pieces in a Tao Lin-ish sort of way — that is, they are so direct yet make me experience an abstract discomfort, a spiritual sluggishness — reading that I realize it may not sound like a compliment, but it is.

also — you can email me at ___@_____.com — I think I am shutting down the XXXXXXX XXXXXX XXXXXXXXX thing."

"i'm glad you liked my writing. zzz maybe this is weird but sometimes I wondered if you would hate it/hate my blog since it could be seen as the self-absorbed narcissism you write about a lot zzz getting writing published felt weird though, and all the attention. I kind of didn't like it. still I asked tao lin if he would be interested in publishing a compilation of my stories/photographs thru muumuu house. zz

will you release a book soon?

plz add me on fb if you want."

"couldn't figure out how to add you on Facebook — I am sort of a Facebook dummy, despite writing about it all the time

maybe you can add me

read your pieces as critiques of narcissism and self-absorption, which are hard to make without embodying them to the nth degree — nothing more narcissistic than complaining about narcissism (like I sometimes do) — think one must feel it in the writing to understand why it is problematic, pervasive, a kind of drugged state

when I used to check on how popular my blog posts and stuff were, I was way more anxious — had a very ambivalent response to knowing what got more attention, and found it too easy to conflate attention to the subject I was writing about with attention to me as a person or writer — can see why those pieces of yours would bring a lot of weird attention, obviously —"

"oh I wanted to ask if you watched the bebezeva documentary and what you thought of it :o also maybe what you think of bebezeva in general??"

"haven't watched but will and let you know —"

Ten days later I booked a flight to New York City. I was technically going to meet my Internet boyfriend, John, a nineteen-year-old who had fallen in love with my writing, and who was paying for everything. But what I was really excited about was the chance to meet Adrien Brody.

I sent him this email:

"hello

I will go to brooklyn may 26 - june 1

I would love to sleep w/ you

probably you're not into that sort of thing but thought I would say anyway zz via nothing to lose

goodluck in your life zzz"

"Hello —

I am intrigued by your proposal — would love to meet up
if possible — Sunday and Monday would be good days
for me — also been meaning to watch bebezeva video —
send me a link to it if you can"

I didn't respond to that message because I didn't know what to say and was terrified of saying something that would make him change his mind.

Four days passed without any correspondence between us. I wanted to keep his attention, so I emailed him again, this time a gallery of photos a friend had taken of me in thigh high socks. I was also curious to see how someone who seemed so dignified and cerebral would respond to a young girl sending sexy photos of herself to him over the Internet.

"here's some art me and some guy made

"provocative yet disarming — not sure if it is supposed to
work this way but I wanted to loop the images and make
them work like animation

I am at this conference session about narrative and
postautonomia marxism, your link oddly resonant with it
"<Call centeredness. Bodies at work, entities in narrative>"

or at least I am forcing a resonance in my mind —

In Amsterdam now but back in New York on Monday —
will plan on seeing you next Sunday —"

I was relieved, and proud, that I was so attractive to him that it made him definitely want to see me.

*

I arrived in New York on Thursday night of the 26th of May. John was a virgin and he lost it to me that night. The rest of the time with him was mostly spent eating out, shopping, laying in bed, and wandering around New York. The entire time was spent half-interested, my mind constantly going back to Adrien Brody.

Then, on Saturday afternoon, after we got back to the hotel (slightly drunk) from Central Park, I checked my email.

"let me know if/when for sun/mon — need to figure out my plans — may be out of town until sun afternoon — hope you are enjoying NYC"

"sunday is fine whenever

you can text me 702-XXX-XXXX

btw sry if too forward

will u read thru my archive of selected blog posts and say what you think

just b/c I want you to"

"will do — be in touch tomorrow 6ish"

John was gone all Sunday visiting a friend.

I spent the day shopping, first at Tiffany's where I bought John a bottle of cologne, meant as an apology for him having to spend so much money on me, and for going off to see another guy. Then later I went to the crowded, five story Forever 21 near Times Square and bought lingerie and nail polish.

I wanted to go for a drink after shopping, but I decided against it and went back to my hotel and lay in my bed, nervously waiting. I checked the time on my phone frequently, near constantly as it got closer to 6.

I tried to read the new book I got, but I couldn't. I could only wonder if I should change my clothes, fix my hair another way, wear my new lingerie…

And then he texted me.

My hands began to tremble.

"Oh my god, oh my god, oh my god, oh my god…" I repeated over and over.

"Back in city. This is Adrien Brody. must determine where
to meet. Where are you?"

I immediately forwarded it to John and closed my phone shut.

I looked at the time it was sent, 6:35. I figured I should wait until at least 6:45 to respond. I put the phone on the bed and inched away, staring at it.

I couldn't tell if I was acting in a contrived way, or if it was all genuine. I thought about that for a while, and then at 6:40 I picked up the phone and typed a response:

"in manhattan. 7th ave and 55th st."

"I can meet you in 45 minutes there and we can proceed out of midtown. I will text you when I get off subway. That okay?"

"k."

I examined myself in the full length mirror in the hotel room, and decided to change my clothes. I decided my legs looked too fat for the shorts I was wearing, so I put on a black pencil skirt and a blue pinstriped dress shirt to match.

I thought that I would meet him near the subway, so I went and stood out in front of the station.

I was worried about my face. I examined my face with my pocket mirror, but I didn't trust it. I took out my phone and took a picture of my face. As I was doing that, someone walked by and made fun of me: "That girl's taking a photo of herself!"

The picture looked horrible. I initially panicked, and then tried to convince myself that it didn't actually look horrible, with mixed results.

I stood in front of that station in a kind of numb anxiety for what seemed like an incredibly long amount of time, made to seem longer by me checking the time on my phone every two minutes. It was a strange feeling, having spent the past two weeks looking forward to nothing but meeting him, but as the minutes drew closer I was overcome with nervous dread. He wouldn't find me attractive, I wouldn't have anything to say, we would sit in a bar in painful silence until he found an excuse to leave and I would feel humiliated and ruminate for months…

My thoughts were interrupted by an incoming text.

"Here. Sitting in dismal space on 56th west of seventh smoking a cigarette by hooters. Where are you?"

"near the 57th st station."

"On the street? What corner. Will find you? Im wearing a blue polo shirt. Bald."

I had to walk away from the station to the nearest street sign to find out what corner I was on.

"west."

I walked aimlessly around the block, looking for "56th west of seventh" or just the sight of him.

I finally saw him on the opposite side of the street from where I was standing.

My first impression of him, after noting that he was bald and wearing a navy polo like he said, was that he seemed awkward and out of place. He was carrying a black shopping bag which added to this feeling somehow. He seemed strange and clumsy. This reassured me, like he was actually what I had imagined and hoped he would be.

I thought he had seen me and would come to me, but he started to turn and walk right.

I texted him just to be sure:

"are you carrying a bag?"

"Yes."

I reached for my phone to text him that he had just passed by me, but I decided to just go up to him instead. I started to run after him. As I started to run, I passed a tourist with his son who said, "Watch out, that girl's going to get you!" This made me feel self-conscious, and so I tripped. My shoe fell off into the street. I covered my face with my hands, embarrassed.

With my head still facing downwards, I went out into the street and put my shoe back on.

I raised my head, and I saw Adrien Brody was looking at me. I could tell he had seen the whole thing.

I walked up to him, feeling humiliated, hoping he would pretend nothing had happened; and that's exactly what he did.

We said hello and started to walk.

I was relieved by the feeling I felt, walking next to him and making small talk. It was a little awkward, but he didn't seem stiff or judgmental like I had terrifyingly imagined him as being.

He told me about how he had been in Pennsylvania earlier that day, and other things about his car.

"It seems like it would be really annoying to have a car here."

He said that it was annoying, but a car is necessary to escape New York, "And sometimes that is everything."

I wondered why he was unhappy living in New York.

"Are you from Las Vegas?" he asked.

I guessed he had realized it from my 702 area code.

"Yeah…but then I moved to Portland for college."

I felt embarrassed that he knew I was from Las Vegas. Whenever anyone asked me where I was from, I always lied and said I was from Portland or Los Angeles. I felt like I was now at a disadvantage, like a hole had been torn in the image I wanted to present of myself.

But then he talked to me about how he used to live there, in the 90's. My mind reeled at the idea of this New York based intellectual having once lived in Las Vegas. At the same time as me, even.

I wanted to change the topic, so I recited the question I had thought of to ask him before we met, "Where are we going?"

He said we were going to take the subway out of midtown, and then he'd try to find a bar that wasn't too loud.

"I like just turned 21, so going to bars is still new to me."

I was dropping my age. I wanted to see how he felt about it.

"Really? Well, going to bars is nice I guess. It gives you somewhere to go…"

His response felt awkward, and I wondered if he felt weird about me being so much younger than him, rather than excited like I had expected and hoped for.

For want of something to do, I reached into my purse and pulled out a cigarette and lit it.

"I'm going to smoke, too," he said and reached for a cigarette.

"I'm so glad you smoke. I thought I was going to have to ask, 'do you mind if I smoke?'"

I really was glad he smoked. It seemed to humanize him more in my eyes. Feeling more comfortable now, I tried to make myself vulnerable to him, to gain his affection.

"I thought you would be like really stiff. I thought this would be like talking to a professor or something. I was like, 'how am I going to impress this guy?'"

"You don't have to impress me! No. I mean, who wants to go through life being that guy?"

I was hoping he would say something to the effect of how my looks made it so he was already impressed by me, which would ease the immense pressure I felt to be interesting and witty (which is what I always hope for from men), but he didn't.

We reached the subway station.

He went through the gate, and I asked him nervously if I could use his Metro Card, as I had lost mine last night.

"Of course," he said, and handed it to me.

We sat next to each other on the train.

I asked if I could take his picture, mainly as an attempt to break the ice.

"Are you going to publish it?" he asked kind of nervously.

"No," I said, fully intending to.

I took and saved the photo. He looked over my shoulder at my phone. When I closed the picture I had taken of him, he saw my wallpaper, which was a picture of a guy from Montreal I had met on my plane ride to New York.

"Who's that?" he asked.

"This guy Ben, I met on the plane to here."

"How'd that happen?"

"Um, we noticed each other while we were waiting to get on the plane. And then he ended up sitting next to me. And…" I started to laugh, embarrassed.

"What?"

"I don't know if it's appropriate to say."

"It's fine. Unless you think it's something the people here couldn't bear to hear," he said, motioning at the people on the train across from us.

"We like made out and kind of had sex."

"What, in the bathroom or something?"

"No, like under the tray tables."

"People fantasize about that…"

"Yeah, Ben said he had fantasized about it. I never really thought about it, I guess."

He told me about how once he had ridden a Greyhound bus across the country, and the woman sitting next to him laying her head on his shoulder, and then gradually groping him.

"I just went along with it…but I kept worrying about the end of the trip. When we both got up, would I have to say, 'Hi, I'm Adrien?' But then when the bus stopped she just got up and left without even looking at me."

I started to laugh really hard, and began to feel comfortable around him, since he had told me such an awkward, sketchy story.

"You must get a lot of like fan letters from girls."

"No, not really."

"Oh, so it must have been ever weirder for you when you got that message from me when I found out I was going to New York."

"I thought it made sense, based on the writing you showed me. Which reminds me, I read that epic blog post you sent me."

I covered my hands with my face, kind of laughing.

"Oh no, I wish you hadn't."

"Why? I liked it."

"It's just, what happened is that I got really drunk in Central Park with the guy I'm here with, John, and when we went back to the hotel for some reason I thought it'd be a great idea to send some long rambling blog entry I wrote to you and Tao Lin and Momus…and then I sobered up and felt so embarrassed. I send Tao Lin so much horrible, unsolicited writing. I think he used to like me, but he doesn't since I kept doing that."

He kind of laughed.

We got off the subway and began walking down a narrow sidewalk past street vendors and Mexican grocery stores.

"What do you think about Tao Lin?" I asked.

"I think he's trying to do something, and what he's trying to do is interesting, but personally I just can't read that stuff. Maybe it's because I'm older…"

"Yeah, when you read it you kind of sink in this malaise. I liked *Richard Yates*, but I don't like his short stories. You liked *Richard Yates* kind of, didn't you?"

"I haven't read *Richard Yates*."

"But you reviewed it?"

"Oh, *Richard Yates*…I guess I did read some of it."

"Do you think Tao Lin is Carles?"

"I think there's a few different Carles. There's one who's really funny and writes those long kind of narrative posts, and I think that's Tao Lin. And there's another one who just sort of knows a lot about indie music, and what he posts is boring to me."

"I don't think Tao Lin writes it…but I do think there are multiple Carles. Because like different posts will be written in kind of different styles, and like the quality varies a lot from post to post."

He nodded.

"Carles put you under his blog BFFs!"

"I thought that was really cool. And also I would write things, and they—I assume it's they—seemed like they were kind of responding to things I wrote which I also thought was really cool."

"You mentioned Momus earlier. Who is that? I've heard the name, but I don't really know who it is," he said.

"Momus is like this Scottish pop singer who was kind of famous in the 80's, like he had this song 'Hairstyle of the Devil' which was a hit, and he had a few other hits. And then in the 90's he went to Japan and produced hits for Kahimi Karie and worked with other Japanese bands who became kind of big in Japan and even the West a little bit. And then he started making kind of like, post-modern songs I guess. And he had this blog, Click Opera, which I don't know, was kind of like your blog is to me. Like I thought it was really interesting because he has this perspective on a lot of things that I had never heard before…so he and his writing and music had a big influence on me and my thought process, so I used to write about him a lot on my blog. And he's really narcissistic, so he has like…"

"He probably has Google alerts for his name."

"Yeah! He has those…so he found out I was writing about him a lot, and he saw that I had written about these rumors I heard about him, like that he was cheating on his long-term girlfriend with an eighteen-year-old girl, and he's like fifty…so he found out and made this song and video about it. And then we started kind of talking and flirting over email. I was really flattered at first, but I don't know, I think he's done that with like hundreds of girls over the Internet, so I don't feel that special anymore," I said, laughing. "I even started kind of seeing the bad parts of him. Like he talked about being in love with this eighteen-year-old girl over the Internet, and he said he 'relates to her searching for an identity.' And it's just like that seems kind of sad, to be like 50 and pining away for some eighteen-year-old girl over the Internet, saying that you share a 'search for an identity' in common with her…"

"That just means you have something in common with everyone on Earth."

"Not me."

"No?"

"No, my personal brand is really well developed."

We laughed.

We reached the bar and went in and sat at the counter.

The bartender asked to see our IDs. I wondered if we looked weird to him, or if it was typical for girls to go to bars with men twice their age in New York.

The bar tender asked what we would have, and both men expected me to order first, but I hesitated, so Adrien Brody said, "I'll have a Sierra Nevada."

"I'll have that, too." I felt silly, but I was too scared to order what I wanted because I was afraid of him judging my beer choice.

"How old are you?" I asked.

"I'm 40."

"That's what I thought."

"Why did you think that?"

"Well, it said on your Facebook profile that you graduated in 1992, so I did the math."

The bartender put our beers in front of us. He paid, and we began drinking.

I found myself just suddenly complimenting him without thinking about it, "I just wanted to meet you because you seemed really smart…"

"Well, prepare to be greatly disappointed."

I laughed.

I asked him about the conference in Amsterdam he said he went to.

He talked about it, and what stood out to me was his frustration:

"Some people knew the blog but I feel like they don't take it seriously because of where it's published. And they didn't take me seriously because I don't have a Ph.D. in sociology or philosophy. But it's like, I'm smarter than these people. The only difference between me and them is that they're teaching…"

"Are you going to write a book?"

He talked about how his friend was pushing him to do it, but how he didn't really have the motivation. He talked more about his friend and his ambition, which he saw as him trying to force onto him. He went on to talk about "the circles that he ran in" and how everyone was always "bragging and self-promoting in that very humble way" and how he felt alienated from it.

"Yes I could never take that. Like when I talk to other writers and they're like so ambitious and always like bragging about getting published in different places and…" I shook my head.

"Do you care about '$n+1$'?" he asked.

"What's '$n+1$'? I've heard of it before but I can't really remember what it is…"

He said he was relieved that it wasn't a big deal to me.

"It's this magazine that's really big in Brooklyn literary circles." He talked about everyone being really excited about it, but him not really caring.

I realized I had only heard of it because I had read an article that he had written for it.

He talked about how his friends were always urging him to move to Brooklyn from Queens, where he lived now.

"It seems like it would be good to not live there and be constantly surrounded by that culture," I said.

"That's what I think. I love where I live…"

I started to talk about being similarly alienated from the intellectuals and activists I knew.

"Like I was involved with socialist politics for a while, but, like when I went to protests or whatever I felt really embarrassed. Like being surrounded by college kids saying things like, 'we're the vanguard of the working class.' I don't think there will be a socialist revolution."

This was the first time I had admitted that to anyone, including myself.

"I don't think there will be either. When I think about leftists I know, like my friend who is pushing me to write a book, I think about how privileged he is…like he says things like, 'I didn't go to an Ivy League, I went to the University of Maryland,' like that means something."

"Are you talking about ___ ___?" He was another writer who wrote in the same places as Adrien Brody whose articles I read sometimes, who I knew enough about to recognize that he was talking about him.

"Yes, ___ ___."

I gasped. "He's only twenty two, right? He's so smart!"

"He's a pretty smart guy."

He went on to talk more about ___ ___, and how aggressive and self-promoting he was, and how seriously he took himself. "But I guess that's what you have to do to succeed…"

"What if ___ ___ led the revolution?" I asked.

"Then…there would be no mercy," he said.

He talked more about "the academic left" and how they acted haughtily towards him. It was surprising and interesting to me, this sense of superiority he talked about, because my experience with regard to the "academic left" had only been in the form of vicious attacks about how they were armchair revolutionaries or fakes who were secretly subservient to power.

I started to feel like I really wanted to sleep with him.

"I feel tipsy already," I lied, so I could have an excuse to start flirting.

But he just said, "Do you need to eat something?"

"Okay," I said, unsure of how to turn that around.

We got up and walked out onto the street, and I followed him as he walked in front of me.

"Does it have to be good food?" he asked.

"No, I eat basically anything."

He talked about how he wanted to go to this diner close by.

"Yeah, don't worry, I've eaten at some pretty gross diners in my time."

I started to smoke another cigarette.

He reached into his bag and pulled out a medicine bottle.

"What's that?"

"Adderall. I thought I would take some so I wasn't exhausted the rest of the day."

"Can I have one?"

"Of course," he said, and gave me one.

I popped it in my mouth.

"Being around you smoking all the time is making me want to smoke a lot more than I should."

"I'm a bad influence on you. But wait, you gave me Adderall, so you're a bad influence, too."

"Mutually bad influences," he said.

He started to talk about past relationships and crushes as we walked.

He talked about an old roommate, who would pick up women and bring them back to his apartment, and after having sex with them, just leave. And he would be left to comfort the girl and "do the emotional work" that hookups/dating entail.

He told another story about a friend of his, and how he was constantly successful with women by just being really domineering, and basically telling them they were going home with him.

There seemed to be this underlying bitterness.

"Do you feel like you resent women for wanting you to be dominating or aggressive when you can't be, or don't want to be?" I asked.

"I've thought about that before. That's kind of putting it strongly…"

"Guys I like are usually like you, and I always have to be really forward and pursue them," I said and smiled, embarrassed.

We reached the diner and stood in front of the entrance.

I looked inside and saw that it was really loud and crowded inside. I was dreading the idea of sitting through a long dinner with him in a place like that.

I took a long drag of my cigarette.

"Are you really hungry?" I asked.

"Yes."

"Do you really want to eat right now?"

"Yes."

I looked away from him and stared out at the street.

"Do you want to go have sex?"

There was a three second pause.

"We could do that."

We started to walk away from the diner and down the street. I was walking really briskly because I was so excited.

"I guess I just don't feel like sitting in this loud diner right now," I said.

"I can understand that."

"How long will it take to get back to your place?" I asked.

"We'll just take a cab." The excitement in his voice was palpable.

He flagged a cab and we got inside and he gave the address to the cab driver.

I slouched down in the seat, and rested my head on his shoulder and grabbed his hand.

He looked at me.

I could feel he was really nervous and excited.

We rode in silence for a while, me laying against him and holding his hand.

"How does that guy you're with feel about you seeing me...?" he asked like he was worried, and I wondered why he cared about what John thought.

"Oh, he doesn't care. He's meeting some girl from Taiwan or something today."

"Oh."

"Are you having second thoughts about me? If we do this, I promise you won't regret it...I'm sorry that probably sounded really stupid," I said and started to laugh. I knew that was an embarrassing thing to say before I said it, but I couldn't stop myself.

He laughed too.

"Because...it's just...I have a girlfriend."

"Oh."

I sat up and turned away, towards the window.

We sat in silence again.

My first thought was that I wished he hadn't told me. I thought it was unfair he was telling me about his girlfriend, and therefore making me partially responsible if we did end up having sex.

And then thinking more, I was surprised he actually had a girlfriend. I thought the frustration he expressed about the difficulty of pursuing women was indicative of him being hopelessly single.

And finally, from reading his articles, besides his intelligence, what I had really admired about his writing was essentially this feeling of how he seemed to uphold human dignity and the sacredness of human feeling and connection. And so it seemed unbelievable that he would cheat. That made me both disillusioned in him, and yet also sexually excited, because he was betraying those values.

"I guess…I was being cowardly in not telling you before. I was afraid you wouldn't meet me if I told you."

I couldn't believe he had actually cared about meeting me. Before we met, I had this feeling like he didn't really care about meeting me, and that I was just kind of an afterthought way in the back of his mind. I felt very flattered at the realization that he wanted to meet me so much that he put effort into hiding things about himself to make sure that I would.

But the feeling of being flattered changed to a sort of abstract feeling of disgust at his lack of respect for his girlfriend, and also for me as he didn't tell me any of this until the last minute, when it was difficult for me to back out.

I wondered if this is just how men are, no matter how feminist and intelligent.

"It's okay. Um, I would be really hypocritical if I judged you for cheating…"

"But it's not about you being hypocritical. It's how you feel about doing this."

"That's true…"

"My hope is just for you to stay in contact with me," he said.

I felt flattered and surprised that he had said that. I hadn't realized he had enjoyed talking to me. And I realized that that was the first time a guy had ever said anything like that to me, that they enjoyed knowing me, even without sex.

I have always been really adverse to the idea of being a "homewrecker," but everything had gone unbelievably well. I couldn't pass up the chance to sleep with my intellectual idol. I knew that I wasn't strong enough to do so, and that I would regret it forever if I didn't sleep with him.

I lay my head back on his chest.

"Are you like really attracted to young hipster girls?"

"Not as like a category…"

"Because I always kind of thought that's why you wrote and followed XXXXXXX XXXXXX XXXXXXXXX and all of those articles about hipsters."

"I wonder if that's what a lot of people think…no, hipsters, like that whole category interests me as a way of living that has always existed in society…"

"Like, when you were younger, were you interested in hipster culture or whatever, but always felt like you were on the outside looking in?"

"Sort of. I always felt like I was on the fringes of it, looking outward, or feeling like I was looking in from the inside somehow."

I was a bit disappointed, because I was sure I had gotten that feeling from his writing. That we had the same fascination with that subculture because we were alienated from it.

The cab reached his apartment, and we walked inside and up two flights of stairs to his door.

When he opened the door, I first noticed his hardwood floors, and then the bookcases that spanned the walls of his apartment. And then I saw his guitar, couch, coffee table, and computer desk.

"Is it everything you imagined?" he asked.

"I never really imagined what your apartment looked like. But if I had had to imagine it, I think this is what I would have imagined."

I walked up to his bookcases and started to examine their contents.

I focused on one near his computer which was full of Marxist books. I examined his volumes of *Das Kapital*.

"Did you make it through *Kapital*?"

"Yes. The first volume, at least…"

"Sorry. I'm really nosy."

"It's okay. That's the first thing I'd do if I was inside someone's apartment."

I looked more.

"Do you notice all the uncracked spines on all of these books I claimed to have read?"

"Can I look on your computer?"

He said yes, so I went and sat on his computer chair and started to click through his pictures and documents. The first thing that caught my eye was a file called "hair." I clicked on it and saw it was full of pictures of a pretty woman with long brown hair. There were several pictures of just her hair. At first I wondered if he had some weird hair fetish, but then I realized that that must be his girlfriend. I was surprised by how pretty she was.

"Who's that?"

"My girlfriend…"

"How old is she?"

"Like mid 30s…"

Seeing those pictures of her made me feel insecure.

"Do you think I'm pretty?"

"Yes. Very much so."

"Do you think I'm smart?"

"What?"

"Sorry, I'm really forward in asking for compliments from people."

"Yes, I think you're very smart. I think it's obvious."

He was standing at my side. I lifted my feet off of his desk and placed them on his shoulders.

"I don't know. Like, I didn't even know who Spinoza was until I read your blog post mentioning him a few days ago."

"You are not alone in that. So many people at that conference barely knew who Spinoza was. Even I have barely read Spinoza."

I started to wonder, and felt relieved that there might be truth to the idea of intellectuals all being frauds. I knew that I certainly was.

"I thought it was funny how you were talking about how people you know are narcissistic and pretentious, and then a few minutes later you were like bragging, 'I'm smarter than these people.'"

He played my remark off. He was busy rubbing my legs up and down.

I looked at my legs. I wondered if he noticed the cellulite on my inner thighs.

"Do you like my legs?"

"I'm crazy about them. Can't you tell?"

"Can I read your email?"

"That's like a big invasion…"

"Okay. I guess it's like the other person didn't consent to it."

"Can I smoke in your house?"

"Let's smoke out front."

"Okay. Do you have any beer?"

I got up and followed him into his kitchen, and he poured me a glass of beer. Then we walked out of his apartment, and stood outside in front of it.

I lit a cigarette, and then started to drink. I quickly downed most of the beer, and as I hadn't eaten all day and am naturally a light weight, was starting to feel pretty drunk.

"Did you cheat before?" I asked.

"Yeah…"

"With who?"

"With this woman in Germany…"

"Do you watch porn?" I asked.

"Yeah…" he admitted guiltily. "I like to think there's this separation between the personal and professional sides of my life. I tend to be into videos of women masturbating…"

"I knew it. Guys like you always are."

"I guess it's just easier to buy into the delusion that they aren't being exploited, with those videos. I can show you some of the sites I look at, if you want…"

His voice sounded weird and I couldn't tell if it was because him showing me the porn he liked excited him, or if he felt awkward that he was talking about his porn habits.

"Sasha Grey," I said.

"I'm not interested in that stuff…"

"I always think it's interesting to hear people's opinions on Sasha Grey."

"I think that you can tell a lot about a person depending on what kind of porn they watch."

"I always thought that, too!" I was excited someone shared my strong held belief about personality and porn habits.

"There's a cop right there," he said and pointed. I looked and saw a cop walking towards us. "What do we do?" I asked, trying to hide my beer and throwing my cigarette to the ground. "We just…" he spun around and pointed towards the door, and we quickly walked back inside of his apartment. I sat down on his computer chair again. I unbuttoned my shirt, revealing my bra. He was standing at my side again. I acted like I hadn't done anything though, and went on Grooveshark and put on music I liked.

"Oh, show me the porn you look at," I said, moving away from the keyboard and mouse.

He got on the computer and typed "sodrained.tumblr.com."

"It's on Tumblr?"

"Yeah. That's where all the best porn is…"

"Sodrained," I said, laughing at the name.

It was all pictures of modelesque brunette women posing. They didn't look like typical pornstars, but they were all very thin and kind of generic looking. And there was the usual feeling of objectification in the photos. So I judged him.

"I'll show you, it's meant to be porn, but I think it's really pretty and expressive."

I went to YouTube and pulled up Aki Hoshino's "Sneaker Lover" video, which for the past two years had been the height of beauty and expression to me, even though it was just meant to be softcore porn.

"Well, there's definitely a feeling of vulnerability…" he said.

He didn't seem to get why I was so moved by it.

I wondered if maybe men are incapable of understanding something like this as anything other than something that's meant to get them off.

"I was really in love with this Irish guy I met in London, he was a photographer and he's 37, but said he was 30 in order to trick young girls he met on the Internet to come meet him, so he could take nude photos of them and have sex with them… It sounds horrible, but he was so interesting and mysterious. I fell really hard for him. I'll show you his blog."

I typed his blog into the address bar, and clicked through the pages, which mostly contained photos of young, naked Asian girls.

"It used to make me so angry and jealous when I looked at his photos… Now I don't really care. But it used to make me angry and sad to the point where I'd cry if I looked at this stuff."

I came upon a photo of him on his blog. He was so tall and thin and blonde.

"Don't you think he's good looking?"

"He just looks like a typical Irish guy to me," he shrugged.

I stood up.

"Can we take a bath?"

"Of course."

I got up and we walked into his bathroom.

He filled the bathtub with water while I took off my clothes. I got in and watched him take off his clothes and then get in the bath. I felt moved by the sight of his legs, which were so long and pale and slender.

I put my knees to my chin.

"One day Tom is showing you XXXXXXX XXXXXX XXXXXXXXX, and then one day you're sitting in Adrien Brody's bathtub."

We both laughed.

"Who's Tom?"

I started to smile. "My old boyfriend. Now he's my best friend. He was the first person to ever love me. Like, I didn't even know it was possible for someone to care about another person that much."

"How many people have you slept with?" I asked.

"I don't keep a list."

"Yeah, but just like estimate."

"Around 15."

"Oh, I've slept with more people than you."

"I figured you were more sexually experienced than me."

"Are you attracted to me, like physically?" he asked.

"Yeah, of course," I said. I didn't actually know if I was or not.

"Are you attracted to me?" I asked.

"Of course," he said.

I gripped my legs tightly and kind of tilted my head to the side.

"I just used to be really insecure about my looks…like for years I felt so ugly I wanted to die."

"I can definitely relate to that."

I was surprised. I didn't know men could feel that way.

I got out and wrapped myself in a towel. I walked into his bedroom and lay on his bed. A moment later he came and lay next to me. I looked across his room, at his desk, which had several bottles of red nail polish on it.

"Why do you have nail polish in your room?"

"It's my girlfriend's. She doesn't live here, but she stays over often enough that she wanted to keep some things here, and that didn't seem like a battle worth fighting…"

"Don't you like your girlfriend?" I asked.

"Of course I like her. She loves me and I love her. But I'm bored…"

I moved my body up to his until our stomachs were touching and my face was buried in his chest.

"Usually I hate talking to people, but I like talking to you." I said. "Like I see talking as a way to get to sex, but I'd rather talk to you than have sex."

"You see talking as a way to get to sex?"

"Yeah."

This was the first time I had admitted that to myself, just talking to him. If I wasn't so drunk I probably would have started to feel really sad.

He held me and stroked my hair.

"I know you think you're weird, but you're not weird…"

I was touched, but I could tell he was talking to himself, or some projection of himself onto me, rather than me.

Still, I was so moved I said, "Can I say something? Something very drunk, and you won't hold it against me?"

He said it was fine.

"I love you."

He was taken aback, but said something nice in reply immediately that I can't remember.

I told him about how I couldn't feel oral sex.

He asked why.

"I can't explain it without telling you way too much about my life."

"But I want to hear it. This isn't about us holding things back or getting uncomfortable."

I just smiled and shook my head.

I wanted to tell him everything, but I didn't. I had too many painful experiences with opening up too much to men, with how they get uncomfortable and run away. All men except for Tom, anyway.

"If I lived in New York, would you date me?"

"I don't know. It's hard to say. You don't live in New York. And we're in very different places in our lives…"

"Men are always like really intrigued by me and want to sleep with me, but they never want to date me…"

"Don't have that be what you take that away from this, that I wouldn't date you…"

I kissed him, and I liked the feeling. It was a very warm and soft kiss.

He moved so he was on top of me. He caressed and then sucked on my breasts. Then he moved to rub his cock between my breasts which was funny to me.

Oh, serious intellectuals are the same as thirteen-year-old boys.

Then he moved his head down until it was between my thighs.

He went down on me for a few minutes, and I faked moaned, pretending to enjoy it.

"Can you like, finger me while you do that?"

So he did, and then I started to enjoy it.

He came up and I kissed him, which I could tell he found exciting.

"Did you like me doing that?" he asked.

"Did you like doing that to me?"

"Yeah, I loved it."

It's hard for two anxious people to have sex. We couldn't ever really relax and enjoy ourselves. We were always worried about what the other person thought of us.

I began to finger myself for a minute, and then I stuck my fingers in my mouth, and then in his.

Then I started to give him a blowjob.

He moaned, almost in a surprised way at first.

Then a minute into it he said, "Can I give you direction?"

"Yeah."

"Slowly, and just the tip. That's the most sensitive part."

"I know," I said and started to slowly run my tongue back and forth around the head of his cock. I liked doing that, but I was surprised. Usually guys are only satisfied when you start gagging on it.

Then he started to move his hips gently up and down so his cock went in and out of my mouth, which I liked a lot. I've never been able to figure out why I get off on being used as an object.

I was surprised he was into mouth fucking.

"Is that okay?" he asked.

"Mm-hm."

"And I guess it's like a porn thing, but when a girl looks up at you it's really hot."

So I shifted my gaze so I was looking up at his face. He looked simultaneously incredibly happy, but also like he couldn't believe what was happening. I was excited that he was watching me.

He facefucked me for a while longer, and then my jaw got sore so I pulled my mouth away and looked at him.

"Do you want to have sex?"

He went to go get a condom, but by the time he was back in the bed and had unwrapped it, he had lost his erection.

It then seemed really strange and unfair to me that the possibility of sex relies on just the one thing, the man's ability to get an erection.

We lay side by side.

He asked me to help him get an erection.

So I moaned, "I want you to fuck me."

He laughed.

I couldn't believe it.

"I can't do it if you're going to laugh at me."

I thought then how it's really unfair how men want and expect you to be really slutty and wild in bed, but they then laugh at you for it. You're either frigid and boring or you're unintentionally funny and crazy.

"I'm laughing but it's also making me hard."

I then just masturbated until he was erect enough to put the condom on.

He penetrated me and I was happy. I felt a strong sexual connection with him.

He started to talk about things.

"I always feel weird talking during sex," I said.

"But that's the best part," he insisted, grinning.

"Let's talk about Gramsci," I said.

"Okay," he said, and we did.

I put my arms around him, my hands resting on his back.

This made him nervous.

"I have a girlfriend. She can't see scratchmarks all over my back."

"It's okay. I bite my nails really short, see?" I said, holding them up to his face.

But I lay my arms at my sides.

"Will you cum in my mouth?"

"Okay, but I probably won't accept it back into my mouth…" (He was making a reference to how I had told him about my friend being into snowballing, and then I had to explain what snowballing was.)

"No, that's gross, I agree."

I didn't actually think snowballing was gross and I really wanted to try it with someone, but I didn't want him to think that I was into things that he thought were gross.

One of us brought up cumming on my face instead.

"I've never done that before…" he said.

He said he would do it, but then said he wouldn't, and he kept going back and forth like this until I rolled my eyes.

"Oh, now you're rolling your eyes at me."

"Well, do you want to do it or not?"

"That's a fair question…"

I looked up at him, feeling vaguely annoyed.

"Okay, I will," he said.

And then a few minutes later he pulled out and took the condom off and was sitting on his knees above the side of my face.

I could tell he was really nervous, and I was afraid he wouldn't be able to cum.

To put him at ease I decided to reenact a scene from a Japanese pornography I had once watched. I opened my eyes and looked into his and smiled up at him.

Then when he finally came on my face I moaned and moved the cum from my cheeks with my finger tips to my mouth, and then sucked my fingers. His face changed to this huge dumb grin, like he couldn't believe it, couldn't believe his luck.

"I feel so vulnerable," he said, his voice shaking.

I felt annoyed that he was only focused on his own feelings, after he had just shot a load on my face.

"Can you take a picture of me with my phone?" I asked.

He got up and got my phone, and then after I told him how to, took a photo. He didn't ask why I wanted a photo, he didn't say anything about it, like I hoped he wouldn't.

"Oh, you can't see anything, it's too dark," I said, looking at the photo.

We talked more about Gramsci, and then our feelings.

My face felt tight as his cum started to dry on my face. I wondered how he could respect me, have this intelligent conversation with me, when I was laying there with his cum all over my face.

So I stood up.

"Come with me," I said, and grabbed his hand and led him to the bathroom.

I wanted to look at myself, but a pink towel was draped over the mirror.

"Why is the mirror covered up?" I asked.

He said it was usually covered up. He talked about how he hated mirrors and looking at himself. I remembered an article he had written about "mirror fasting," and how it ended it with "what seems to be called for is mirror fast after mirror fast."

I turned the sink on and rinsed my face off. I then took hand soap from the counter and rubbed it all over my face. I was afraid of the hand soap drying out my skin, but I was more afraid that he would think I was gross if I didn't wash my face off with soap.

"Oh, you have a hickey on your neck," I said after I dried my face off.

"I was worrying earlier you did something that gave me a hickey…did you do it on purpose?"

"No, I didn't! I swear to God! I had no idea that I was doing anything that might give you a hickey!"

He seemed convinced that I hadn't done it on purpose by my anxiety.

"I guess it looks like it could just be a zit or something," he said.

We went and lay down in his bed again.

"Was I like how you thought I would be in person?" I asked.

"Well, I figured you would be inward and quiet, and that I would have to talk a lot."

"I'm sorry I made you do all the talking."

He said it was okay.

"Did you look at my Facebook?" I asked.

"No."

"Why not?"

"Because I don't look at anyone's Facebook…"

He went on to talk about how he was afraid not using Facebook made him a loser. I thought back to the first thing that I had read by him that had really made an impact on me, when he wrote about how he would literally cover his face with his hands when going on Facebook because of all it meant with regards to self-promotion and commodification of self.

Then he went on to ask me if I understood something about talking to people and wondering why they should care, and what the point was, but I didn't really understand what he was getting it. And then I told him how there were a lot of times I couldn't bring myself to care about my friends when something bad happens to them, but he didn't understand.

We talked more, and then we watched *Annie Hall* for a while.

Then we started to fool around, but he was out of condoms.

We went to Duane Reade to buy more condoms. While walking to get them, we passed the cosmetics section. I grabbed onto his arm in order to stop him, and then picked up a hand mirror and held it in front of our faces.

"We look cute together," I said, and was happy when he agreed.

He bought a three pack of condoms, cigarettes, and a candy bar.

We went back to his house, and lay down together on his couch.

I picked up a book called *Intern Nation* that was laying on his coffee table.

"I have to read that. I'm not looking forward to it," he said.

I thought it was funny because I always think back to this joke on Hipster Runoff about how unpaid internships are the contemporary version of slavery, and here was a book apparently about that for real.

"Will you feed me a Reese's peanut butter cup?" I asked as I put the book down.

"Of course," he said, unwrapping the candy bar he bought.

I opened my mouth and he placed the whole disk in my mouth. I chewed it and swallowed it quickly, grossed out by how sweet it was.

"Yucky," I said and wiped my tongue off with my hand.

He said it was a bad idea to eat chocolate when you haven't eaten all day.

I got up and lay on his bed again and he followed me.

We started to make out again, and then he started to finger me.

"You feel very wet."

He was excited by this, and put a condom on right away.

"Do you want me to be on top?"

"No, I like being on top."

"But guys like you always love girl on top."

He insisted again he liked being on top.

I wanted to ask why, but I didn't for some reason. I made a note to ask him later, but never did. I had never met a guy who liked doing it in missionary before. I kind of even trained myself out of liking it, because most guys are so bored by it.

I felt very connected to him, like before, and enjoyed having sex with him very much.

He came inside me, and lay on top of me for a while. I liked the feeling of his warm cum pooled at the tip of the condom inside of me.

We lay like that in silence for a while.

"It's very different when you cum like this," he said.

I wanted to say, "This is how you're supposed to cum, right?" But I didn't for some reason.

He got up and threw the condom away, and then we cuddled, our eyes closed.

"I'm afraid to go to sleep," he said.

"Why?"

"I'm afraid of losing the connection, I guess."

If you're afraid of losing our connection just because we went to sleep it's not like it was very strong in the first place...

We did eventually fall asleep.

In the morning we got up and I used his toothbrush and he showered and then we got dressed and split his last Adderall.

We smoked out front of his apartment.

He wanted to go for a drive so we did.

We drove around for a long time. We talked about Joan Didion and when he taught English composition courses.

I asked him if he was ever attracted to his students and he said, "There would always be some...I hated it when they would try to make it about that..."

We reached an empty beach and we walked to the shore. The sky was all grey, but he said that it probably wouldn't rain until later in the day.

I took my heels off and carried them in my hands.

"Will I like step on a needle or something?"

"It's fine."

We sat by the shore.

"I really need you to hold me right now," he said.

I lay on top of him.

He talked about how he used to feel like male subjectivity is false while female subjectivity is true….

I have had a lot of experience with some men, who want to otherize women and make them out to be somehow pure or in a way "better" than men, but still not quite human. I could see him being that type, and felt glad he wasn't anymore.

We lay there in silence until it was interrupted by my phone beeping. I checked it, and saw I had received a text from the boy I was staying in my hotel with, John.

He was wondering if I was okay. I responded that I was fine and missed him and would see him later today.

"What was that?" Adrien Brody asked.

"Oh, it was John."

"Do you have to go back to your hotel?"

"No, I think he just wanted to know that I'm not dead."

He asked me more about John.

"He has like really unrealistic expectations of what people will do. Like you know how Tao Lin was selling a bunch of his stuff on ebay a little while ago?"

"Yeah."

"He bought it for me, he spent like $250 because he thought Tao Lin would let him pick it up in person, and then we could go together and meet Tao Lin."

He talked about how Tao Lin probably has a lot of people trying to get too close to him and so was very cautious.

"And just like, I feel like he wants me to be this manic pixie dream girl archetype that I just can't be."

"Like Amélie?"

"Yeah."

"I feel like so much of life is about getting past that, seeing idealized versions of people. No, it's definitely better to see the real person…"

"Yeah. He has this weird idealized image of me. Like he called me a 'genius' and I think he thinks by associating with me he can become a part of what he calls 'the Internet writing subculture' which I'm not even a part of…I feel like he's just trying to use me because he thinks I'm living this weird alternative life, and he's afraid of ending up an engineer living in the suburbs. But he is studying engineering at Dartmouth and is working as a businessman. I think he should just accept his life like that."

He talked about "selling out" and other things.

"I don't know. I feel kind of bad that I'm using him. I mean, John makes all of his own money, and I live off of my parents. I don't have any right to judge him."

"Using him how?"

"To go to New York. He paid for the hotel room and bought me a ton of drinks and gifts and all of my food and everything. And then later to go to China."

"You're going to China?"

"Yeah, he works in China, and he said I could live in his apartment near Shanghai with him."

"Well, he's probably getting as much out of buying you things as you are," he shrugged.

We lay there talking more, but then it started to thunder and incredibly heavy rain poured down. We got up and ran, holding hands, to get shelter under a roof nearby. This worked until the wind started to blow the rain at us.

He stood in front of me and put his hands on my shoulders, acting as a barrier to protect me from the rain.

I felt strange that here we were two leftist feminists I guess, and of course the feeling was that we had this unconventional relationship, a way of treating each other, but here now when it was pouring down rain he automatically fell in the role of being a man and shielding me from the rain.

"We should just run for it," I said.

"Are you sure?" he asked.

"Yeah," I said.

We ran back to his car.

On the way I got soaking wet; my hair was dripping as if I had just gotten out of the shower.

We sat in his car with the heater and windshield wipers on for a while. Then he asked me if I was hungry. I said a little bit, so we drove to a diner in his neighborhood.

He ordered eggs and bacon, and I ordered a Greek omelette.

I felt sick when this huge omelette was placed in front of me by the waiter.

I tried to pick at it, but every bite was a struggle.

"I'm usually like a vacuum, I don't know why I don't feel like eating," I said.

"It's probably the Adderall."

"Oh."

We left and drove back to his apartment.

I went and lay down on his couch, and instead of lying next to me he went over to his computer.

"Why are you over there?" I asked, my voice needy and whiny.

"I'm just…checking my email."

"Come back over here."

So he did and I sat up and hugged him.

I held him for a while in silence.

"Can we go back to my hotel so I can change my clothes?" I asked.

"Of course."

"I'll have to text John and tell him to leave for a while…"

"Are you sure? I can wait on the street."

"No. I really want you to see my hotel room. Is that weird?"

"I want to see your hotel room."

I was really happy that he wanted to, and that he implied he wanted to spend the rest of the day with me.

"Do you want to have sex in your hotel room?" he asked, grinning.

"No, that's kind of fucked."

"I can see why you would think that…"

I wondered why men are so turned on by cheating.

I texted John that I would be back to the hotel room with Adrien Brody in about half an hour, and could he please leave until I texted him? And that I was really sorry and would make it up to him later.

Almost instantly he replied, "I suppose so."

I felt really guilty.

"I feel bad kicking John out of the hotel room that he paid for…"

"Will he get mad at you?"

"No. Like he thinks I'm really exciting, and he probably just sees this as an extension of that…"

"I can understand how he finds you really exciting."

I wondered if he misunderstood "exciting" to mean "sexually exciting," and I hoped he didn't.

We got into his car and he started to drive from Astoria to Midtown.

I saw that his iPod was connected to the car stereo, and so I looked through his songs.

He said his iPod was very classic rock based, and it was. I was also surprised by some of the bands he had on it, like U2.

"I thought your iPod would be like more hipstery…"

I wanted to play Belle and Sebastian, but I was too embarrassed to, so I played France Gall then Serge Gainsbourg, and then Felt.

"Is this Felt?"

"Yeah."

We drove in silence listening to music.

When we arrived into Midtown I gave him directions to the hotel. After he parked I led him to the entrance.

"You're staying at the Hotel Wellington?" he asked.

"Yeah. John picked it out."

He talked about how he used to get coffee and lunch there every day when he was working a job in the area, and about how the staff at the cafe inside once knew his name and his order by heart.

I texted John that we were there.

He responded to give him 15 minutes to get out because he had just gotten out of the shower.

I didn't want John to see us on his way out of the hotel, so I grabbed Adrien Brody's hand and led him to the bar next door to the hotel.

"Let's hide in here," I said.

We sat at the bar.

The bartender greeted us and asked what we would have.

"Can I have a Bloody Mary, please?" I asked.

"I'll just have orange juice."

"Can I see your ID?" the bartender asked.

I handed her my passport.

She stared at it for a while.

"Oh, you're not…oh, no, you are 21. I'm sorry," she said, and smiled and handed my passport back to me.

I felt embarrassed that I had ordered booze and he was just having juice. And I was surprised to learn that you could order juice at a bar.

The bar was mostly empty, so we got our drinks very quickly.

We mostly sat in silence, but it wasn't uncomfortable.

I drank my Bloody Mary very quickly, absent-mindedly.

"Was that good?" he asked, kind of taken aback.

The bartender also seemed taken aback and asked me if I wanted another one.

I said no, feeling embarrassed.

John texted me that he had left the hotel, so Adrien Brody paid for the drinks and we walked to the hotel and then rode the elevator up to my room.

As I opened the door, I apologized for the mess. The floor was covered in my clothes and packaging from gifts John had bought me.

"John hates how messy I am."

"It's a small room, but being lazy in your hotel room is what it's all about…" he said.

I lay on the bed, tired. He lay next to me. We lay like that in silence for a while, and I wanted to for a long time, but I realized I had better hurry and change so I didn't kick John out for too long.

I stood up and undressed, and then went to the bathroom and washed my face and then started to brush my teeth.

I walked from the bathroom to the bed and sat naked on top of Adrien Brody while brushing my teeth.

"This is like that 'Sneaker Lover' video," he grinned, referring to a scene in it where Aki Yoshino brushes her teeth in lingerie.

When I was done brushing my teeth, I went to go rinse my mouth out.

Then I told Adrien Brody to turn around and look at the wall until I said it was okay.

He complied, and I picked the black lace lingerie bodysuit John had bought me from American Apparel the other day off the chair it was laying on and put it on.

I told him to turn around, and then I sat on his lap.

"This is too good," he said.

I kissed him and we made out for a while, and then I stopped and got dressed into clean clothes and brushed and straightened my hair and did my makeup.

I decided I wanted to shop for clothes for him.

We left the hotel, and I texted John that we were gone.

We walked aimlessly around Midtown, looking halfheartedly for men's clothing stores. Nothing seemed to suit him.

We walked mostly in silence, holding hands.

I talked about how I had gone shopping at Forever 21 a few hours before our date. He told me about an article he was writing about Forever 21 and fast fashion in general, and how the editor he sent it to criticized him for ignoring female subjectivity/"the female shopping experience."

"I always thought that Forever 21 was a really stupid name for a store."

"It kind of encapsulates the whole fast fashion philosophy. Like you're only as old as the latest fashion you're wearing…"

Weeks later I would read the article about fast fashion he talked about, and when I saw that the opening line was, "I have always thought that Forever 21 was a brilliant name," I wondered if he had written that in response to what I had said.

After a while we gave up the pretense of finding clothes for him and just sat on a bench in Central Park and smoked.

I felt like a lot of people were giving us dirty looks. I couldn't tell if it was for smoking or for him being twice my age.

I asked if he wanted to go to American Apparel.

He said okay, and that he had never been there before.

I was surprised because it seemed like he endlessly referenced American Apparel in his writing.

I asked him if he got turned on by American Apparel ads. He said sometimes but that he didn't see them much lately since he wasn't looking at Hipster Runoff much these days.

We walked hand in hand to American Apparel. We got lost on the way and had to double back a few times.

We weren't greeted when we walked in, which was a new experience for me.

I'm always struck by, at least to me, the beauty of the interior of American Apparel stores.

"Am Appy," he said, looking around.

I led him upstairs to where most of the men's clothes were.

He made fun of the packaging on the clothing, especially the packaging for a bowtie which had a picture of a blonde woman wearing a v-cut black leotard and a bowtie around her neck.

"She's going to an audition."

We looked through racks of clothing. I could tell he wasn't interested in anything. Finally he said, "I don't think I can wear anything here."

"Poor Adrien Brody, so out of his element despite writing about American Apparel all of the time."

The "I'm Going to be a Supermodel" song started to play on the store radio and he said, "The music alone is worth writing about."

We left the store and started to walk back to the hotel. It was around 2 PM. He said that he should probably get going to his friend's birthday party that he had mentioned he had to go to earlier today.

We walked in silence for the rest of the time back to the hotel.

I started to feel very sad when we reached the entrance.

We embraced for a long time.

Finally he said he would text me later tonight.

I walked into the hotel and he started to walk down the street towards his car.

I went up to my hotel room and flopped on the bed, exhausted.

John was there, sitting on the other side of the bed.

"How was it with that guy?" he asked.

I sighed.

"It was really good, actually. I feel like, we are like…the same person."

"Really?"

He gave me a *maneki-neko* coin bank and candy he had bought for me in Chinatown.

I ate the candy and kissed him.

I felt anxious, thinking that now that I had fallen hard for Adrien Brody, I would be even less willing to put effort into the already strained relationship I had with John. I realized how truly tepid my feelings for John were, and how disconnected I felt from him, now that I had Adrien Brody to compare him to.

And indeed, that afternoon and night I spent with him consisted of uncomfortable silence that finally culminated in fighting with him. I felt relieved when he left New York the next morning to go back to work. And I was happy because I had our hotel room to myself for the last day that I was in New York.

Early in the morning, right after John had left, I texted Adrien Brody.

"John saw us coming back to the hotel. He said you look really tall and gangly."

                                        "He left out gap toothed."

"John had to leave to go back to work, and so I have the hotel room to myself until tomorrow afternoon. Will you come over?"

He replied that he worked until 10 at night and would come over when he got off work.

I slept most of my last day in New York. I felt pathetic, but I was very tired and nothing seemed appealing. I just wanted to see Adrien Brody again. I thought and wrote about him when I wasn't asleep.

At around 6 PM I texted him.

"Are you still coming over tonight? JW."

"Yes. Why do you ask?"

"JW."

Then around 10:30 he texted me that he was at the hotel and asked which room. I texted him the room number and decided to change my clothes. Just as I was fully dressed, he knocked.

I cracked the door open.

"Sorry it's messy."

There were still clothes and packaging and books strewn all over the floor.

"It's alright. I saw it before…"

I opened the door all the way and he came in.

We lay down on the bed together.

I didn't look at him, I just lay against him with my eyes closed.

We lay in silence until he said, "Did you get into a fight with John last night?"

He knew because I had written an entry on my blog about it.

"Yeah. He read and wrote in my notebook. So I grabbed his Blackberry and threw it at the wall."

"I bet he wasn't happy about that…"

"He didn't really seem to care. He was more worried because I was mad at him. But like, I had never been that angry in my life."

"Why were you so mad? Was it just the invasion of your privacy?"

"It was that, but it was more like that he wrote in my notebook that made me mad. It felt like such a violation."

He didn't seem to understand.

"Do you always wear blue?" I asked, looking at his work shirt.

"Most of the time. Do you think it's a good color for me?"

"I guess…"

I started to hold onto him really tightly.

I was working up the courage to say what had been going through my mind since we met.

"I feel weird about having sex with you," I said.

"We don't have to do that anymore."

"It's not the sex really, it's more like, like…I don't wanna say."

He urged me to tell him, and that it would be okay.

"It's like, how much can you really care about and respect other people when you're cheating on your girlfriend with me?"

"I think that's a fair criticism to make, that I have no integrity."

"And I feel like you really want to feel connected to someone, so you're like forcing this connection on to me rather than there like genuinely being a strong connection between us."

He sighed and said that could be true, but that he felt more like he could connect with me only because he knew that I would be gone soon.

"You don't want to see me again?"

"I don't know. We're at very different places in our lives…"

"The fact that you're unsure means we won't."

"Well, I'm here now."

He was.

"I was naive to think that this wouldn't happen…I guess I was hoping you would just use me. We're messing with dangerous things here. Who are we to do that?"

I didn't understand.

"Do you feel weird about me being twenty one?"

"No. You're an adult," he shrugged. "Should I feel weird about it?"

"No, I was just wondering if you did."

I was actually trying to explore my reverse Lolita complex with him, but I backed off after that because it seemed he wasn't into it at all.

"Were you attractive when you were younger?" I asked.

"I didn't think so but I'm not the best judge of that….I had long hair…"

I started to laugh really hard. Him having long hair really added to the picture I had often imagined of him before we met, of him standing around feeling awkward at indie rock shows in college.

"Were you?" he asked.

"No. Like I got bullied a lot in school because of my looks."

"That doesn't mean you were unattractive."

"No, I was. Like I was kind of fat and I had acne…I wonder what would have happened to me if I hadn't gotten attractive. I'd be dead now, probably."

"Really?"

"Yeah."

I talked about how mean I felt I had been treated throughout my life for my looks. And how I felt like people judged me less now that I was attractive. How even though it's not true, I can't get the idea out of my head that I feel safer when I look pretty. How I felt like the defining theme of my life has always, always been the way I look.

"It's interesting because people always talk about how women manipulate men with their beauty and have all this power because of their physical attractiveness and ability to have sex or withhold sex from men, but I've always felt like my own physical attractiveness is just like a defense from men. I feel like men have all of the power, and they attack you if you aren't attractive. And even men who are attracted to me, I feel like they have all the power because they get less emotionally invested in me than I am in them. But maybe I would have more of that power people talk about if I were more conventionally attractive," I said.

I liked to talk about these things with him because I could tell he was fascinated by female beauty, and what it meant.

"I guess that it depends on what you mean by power and what you want to gain with that power," he said

He asked me what personality flaws I thought people judged me by.

"Oh, I don't know…Sometimes I get called a sociopath."

"Do you think you're a sociopath?"

"No. I get called that a lot, but I don't think of myself that way."

"No, you don't seem like that."

"I think 'sociopath' is just what really controlling people call other people when they don't do what they want," I said.

"That seems about right."

"I guess also I'm really voyeuristic, and it gets me into trouble. Like I don't respect people and their privacy as much as I maybe should. And sometimes I keep like drilling people for information about themselves even when they get uncomfortable because I'm so fascinated by other people I want to know everything about them, and I feel this drive to write about them."

"How are you voyeuristic?"

"Like how I wanted to look through your computer and read your emails."

"I want to meet Momus soon, but I'm afraid he won't like me in person."

"Why wouldn't he?"

"I guess he just thinks I'm really smart and interesting and exciting," I said and started to smile.

"But you are."

I realized I was smiling because I realized that I did think I was all of those things.

But I shook my head.

Because it's a lot easier to fall back on pretending that I'm still insecure than to actually present myself as someone who believes they have all these great qualities, since it leaves me open to being cut down, which it seems like people are dying to do.

"No. I come off as really cool on the Internet for some reason."

"You don't think you're really cool?"

"No, I'm really shy and awkward."

"Well, I think that you are pursuing this way of living…" That's very genuine and honest, he went on to say.

He said he admired me for "being upfront about your awkwardness. I wish I could go back to being young and do that."

"You're going to admit that I'm awkward?"

"I think…you're a little awkward. I think I'm very awkward."

"I know. Even Tom who loves me and always sees the best in me always makes fun of me for being awkward," I said, smiling.

"Tom was your old boyfriend? The one who loved you?"

"Yeah. He was the first person to like see me as like an actual human being instead of like…like…"

"Some mystical nymph?"

"Yeah."

"So why did you break up?"

"Because I didn't love him."

"I guess that is important…"

"Meeting you started off really awkward and embarrassing, when I was running towards you and my shoe fell off."

"I thought that was so endearing. I took that as a good sign. That was just how I wanted this to go."

I felt so surprised, and relieved, that someone could find my awkwardness "endearing." I had never even imagined that it could be something that someone liked, or even accepted about me. "I guess that's why most of my friends are guys. They just are like more accepting of awkwardness for some reason."

He talked about how women are socialized to do the social work of putting people at ease in conversations, and how they expect other women to help them with that, and when they don't they get put out.

I brought up an article he had written since the first time we met, about young girls on the Internet who were pressured by the Internet's "attention economy" and the way social media is arranged to exploit them by using their sexuality to get attention. I asked if he thought I was like that.

He said that talking to me definitely made him think more about female subjectivity, but that he thought that what I did wasn't like Kiki Kannibal, but that "what you do seems more in line with that video you showed me of that female artist who posed for porn herself because she didn't want to exploit other women," he said, referring to a video of Cosey Fanni Tutti I had sent him.

I felt relieved.

Then I asked him the other thing I was worried that he thought about me, that I was afraid he saw me as commodifying and exploiting myself on Facebook, like he was constantly writing about.

"No. I'm not talking about people who are aware of it. It's just like people who write status updates 'today me and Susie went to the beach…' It's just, don't you think there should be more than that tying people together?"

I wondered if only people like us who had been disconnected from others our whole lives could be concerned about that sort of thing.

"What do you think of those feminists on the Internet who think that pornography is ruining intimacy?" he asked.

"Yeah, that's what I think, actually."

"I just think it changes the terms of intimacy, like intimacy can be found in doing things that you wouldn't see in porn videos…"

"I can already see it, when I have sex with young guys. Their whole idea of what sex is has been shaped by pornography. They're bored by sex that isn't like violent or degrading, or they think that sex has to be that way."

"I guess it's different if you grew up watching it."

He talked about how he remembered when Internet pornography first became big, and how he was thinking about what would happen to the industry now that there wasn't money involved. He was hopeful then, but now he felt that it seems like people are happy to just perform like before, except for free.

I talked about the disillusionment I had with the Left in regards to pornography.

"It's just funny to hear leftist guys one day talking about the evils of wage slavery, and then the next day defending porn based on 'women's autonomy.'"

He kind of laughed, "Don't they see something wrong with how women are supposedly showing their autonomy with the way they act in porn?"

Then I talked about how I was suspicious of third wave feminism and even leftists who had embraced "feminist porn" and things like stripclubs as "empowering."

"I feel like that sort of thing is feminists giving up and just trying to like change the terms of their exploitation," I said.

"I guess that's the whole criticism of Slutwalk," he said.

"Yeah, that's kind of how I feel. But at least something vaguely feminist is happening, I guess." I sighed.

"I think the main problem with sex work is how it's romanticized. It's not this mystical Belle du Jour experience. We just need to realize it's just another worker being exploited by capital and unfair property arrangements," he said.

"I can see where they're coming from, since sex workers have been portrayed as less than human for so long that you'd kind of want to like honor them, but…"

I wondered if I should talk about my own experiences with sex work, or if that would be uncomfortable.

I talked to him about my writing, and how I was afraid to publish it.

"I feel like they would edit my writing so it would be technically better, but less honest and expressive."

"Yeah, but I think you can find a balance between those things."

"But I'm not interested in a balance."

"I guess that's legitimate…"

And I talked about how all of the competition and ambition made me sick.

"I wish I could just show my writing and pictures I take of myself to a lot of people without all of the other things that come along with writing to write. Like all of the competition between writers bragging about how they were noticed by whatever important person, and bragging about how they've gotten published in so many places. And all of the ambition that they talk about, like how they want to become rich and famous through writing…"

He listened, but I was disappointed when he didn't seem to understand that I wasn't afraid to compete or be ambitious, but that I just didn't want to.

I lay on his chest.

"Are you an idealist or a materialist?" I asked.

"A materialist I guess…I assume you're a materialist, that goes along with Marxism."

"Yeah," I said, smiling, happy that he was a materialist, too.

We started to make out and we took off our clothes.

We didn't have any condoms.

"Do you wanna just do it?" I asked.

"I don't want to get you pregnant…"

"You can just pull out."

"Yeah, but…"

"It's okay. Like I get tested all the time and I don't have anything."

I was really desperate to have condomless sex with him, to become totally connected with him.

"I wish…that it didn't have to be that way."

And I knew that was the last word on the matter.

I asked if I could go home with him, and then take a cab home tomorrow morning.

"No. That's too much."

I was both surprised and not to hear that from him.

Here it is, what I'm used to from men.

"Can't we just go and buy condoms then?"

"That's a good idea…"

So we got up. I tucked my shirt into my shorts and he nodded in approval. Men respond much more to hot pants than miniskirts. I had no idea until wearing them for the first time in New York.

I looked at myself in the elevator's metal reflection.
"I look really stupid right now," I groaned.
"No you don't."

We walked a few blocks to Duane Reade.
"What time is it?" I asked.
"About 3 AM." I gasped, "You're joking."
"No."

We got there and he got condoms, and I asked him to buy me beer so we got a six pack of Stella Artois.
We got in line, but I slipped outside while he bought them, embarrassed for some reason to be seen buying condoms with him in the middle of the night.

On the way back to my hotel we walked past a produce vendor on the street.
I thought no one was watching it, so I grabbed an avocado.
"You have to pay for that," Adrien Brody said.
I turned my head backwards and saw the vendor nodding.
"Oh. I thought he wasn't around."
He went over and paid for the avocado for me.
I really liked the image of him taking three dollars out of his wallet and handing it to the vendor for me.
We started to walk again.
"This isn't ripe. I didn't even want it, I just felt like stealing an avocado."
I put it in my purse.

We got back to my hotel room and sat on my bed.
"I'm going to have to leave right after we do this," he said.

I started to drink a bottle of Stella.
"Do you need to be drunk to—" he started.
"No."
"You didn't even need me to finish that sentence."

We started to take off our clothes again.
"Is this alright?" he asked.
"No, but, 'this is the life I have chosen.'" I said, quoting him from when he had talked earlier about living a boring white collar life.

"I feel like…I haven't ever met someone I was able to talk to like I can talk to you. The way I always wanted to talk to people, like the way that I think and write. And I feel like we're very similar and I've never met someone like me before. Do you feel like you've met someone like you before?" I asked.
He shook his head.
"No, I haven't, except for you. But I don't know what it means."

I lay down on the bed and he lay down on top of me.
"I want to get you out of your head," he said.

We started to have sex and I was overcome.

This is it. This is what sex is. What I've spent the past three years of my life, my entire adult life, looking for, even though I hadn't realized it until now.

"That's the most incredible thing I've ever seen."

"What is?" I asked, though I knew.

"Your face right now."

I was vaguely aware my eyes were open very wide.

"Do you want to know something? This is the best it's ever felt for me," I said.

"Because I'm going slow?"

"No." I felt put out that he would try to reduce it to that.

"I feel like this is the most that sex can ever be," I said.

I meant it in a positive way, but he agreed and was instead disappointed. He said that he hoped for "some feeling of transcending bodies."

"What does this mean for you?" he asked.

"I don't know. Maybe I'll get really bored of sex after this."

"Will you lift your arm up?" I asked. It was blocking the side of his face.

"Is it squashing you?" he asked and did.

It wasn't good enough; his head was too close…

"And will you move your head up a little bit?"

He did and so his face was now about a foot above mine and there was nothing in the way.

I slapped him in the face.

"Ow!"

I started to laugh really hard.

I wish I could say that I did it for a more dignified reason: that I wasn't going to let him use my body for his pleasure, some fake imagined emotional connection that he was forcing in his mind onto us…but really I was just sad and angry about how he was going to leave after we had sex, that he wouldn't let me go home with him earlier.

But then my laughing died down and tears started to well up in my eyes.

"Oh, no. I don't want to be that person who cries during sex."

"Why not? It's really common…"

Is it? I stopped trying to fight the tears and just started to cry.

I could feel him lose his erection.

"Why are you crying?"

"I don't know."

"Because you're feeling sorry for yourself?"

That was his counter-attack. A verbal slap in my face.

"I feel like you're the one who has all the power here," he said.

"You're the one who wants to leave in a few minutes. That's why I hit you, because I was sad that you have all the power."

"Yeah."

"I hit the last guy I had sex with, too, because I was sad he didn't want to date me. It's like that again. Hitting you didn't make me feel better or change anything. It's not like I can stop you from leaving."

I'm totally powerless in the face of men.

He pulled out and threw the condom in the waste bin and started to get dressed.

For the first time, I looked closely at his face as he was getting dressed. I realized that he was actually very attractive, just in a strange way. Or a complex way, rather, where you had to look at him for a while and think about it.

"I'm going to say something, and don't say it's not true. I'm never going to connect with anyone."

"I think that's very fatalistic."

He finished dressing and I lay in the bed naked and quietly crying.

"I know you said you don't want me to say this, but you will connect with someone one day. It's just not going to be me."

It was nice, and I wanted to believe it, but I knew that he didn't know, and that he was just saying that because it was what he should have said right then.

We hugged and kissed and he headed towards the door.
"Goodbye," he said.
"Bye."

He went out the door, stuck his head in again, and then he was gone.

*

She works under an assumed name. She once wished she were in Japan, but now she subjects her fascination with Japanese culture—its preoccupation with reified cuteness, with fastidiousness, with compliant femininity—to elaborate scrutiny, with a variety of unconventional tools: submersion, revulsion, role-playing, obsession, ridicule, mimicry. She writes with a stark and troubling ambivalence. It can be easily misread as apathy, numbness; this is part of what she risks. An elaborate strategy of purification, to blend honesty and revulsion until they are no longer separable, until readers must begin to shut down themselves. She is sure enough of herself to confront and even invite misunderstanding, as though misunderstanding might offer a way forward toward an authenticity beyond the deceptive surfaces of exhibitionism.

criticism

"It bothers me that anyone would consider this scenario remotely compelling—a young girl desperate for attention and validation solicits a random, married writer twice her age in a position of relative authority for sex, he cums on her face (easily one of the most degrading sexual acts, and one heavily influenced by porn culture), she writes about it in awful prose that's borderline pornographic, and you manage to find something redeemable from it all."

The fascinating thing about [...] alloway's stories are not that they are [...] But that they are stories about a female train-wreck, a creeper, a woman that gets obsessed with boys and her looks, and who lacks any moral component. Her female characters are so fucking ugly we have to keep looking...There is just something exciting about a pathetic person being the star of a story.

oh no of course not she's just being a brave feminist writer being courageous enough to write in as obscene a way as men and why the heck shouldn't she and she's highlighting the pornification of women and rape culture and doing that in the most unflinching and candid way possible and she portrays a delicate, vulnerable, young woman and blah blah fucking blah

when women are only getting 'relevant' in alt lit because of nudity and talking about fucking completely artlessly it is made even harder for women in alt lit to be listened to

i wrote a poem about sex a week ago.

maybe i should have linked a picture of my tits with it and wait patiently for some alt lit zine to spend paragraphs and paragraphs defending my case

admittedly when gabby gabby was in the "alt-tits" scandal she was vilified for it and i am happy to admit i was one of the people who was pretty outraged.

why does nobody call marie calloway out on this shit? what gabby gabby did compared to this was tame as heck.

sorry, no, don't like this. stop it now marie you're embarrassing yourself.

i want marie calloway to make a big salad

a big leafy salad

and as she's reading her yahoo articles and reblogging girls that she wants to look like on tumblr and contemplating posting a shitty facebook status

i want her eyes to become wide

i want her to have a surprised facial expression

i want her to be choking to death on kale leaves

i want marie calloway's body to slam to the floor, also causing blunt head trauma

i want the cops to come and investigate and i want them to say 'really?' when they see her body

i want her body to be cold in the morgue

i want people to make an 'in memoriam facebook page' for marie calloway

i want the cover photo to be kale."

Dear "Marie Calloway,"

When I was 21, Britney Spears was a Musketeer. I was insecure with a vo[...]ive and compliments, particularly, the admiration of older men. I ached to be a[...] for money. When I started stripping, Tao Lin was ten years old. This was before FB, YouTu[...] phones and before the send button became a lethal weapon. This was before celebrity sex t[...] a nation obsessed with gawking at the horrific unraveling of the human spirit on 60 inch Plasm[...]. I was 21, and I knew what time it was. Time to use my feminine whiles to c[...]ive. I explored the shit out of my sexuality and smeared it all over bathroom walls and lesbian m[...] my stinking fingers to fisting parties, spied on my girlfriend who'd broken into my house and he[...]ead and fucked me. I ensnared a slave. I'd try anything.

You know you're pretty. Thin legs and luscious hair, the pictures of your glossy lips surrounded by fog. I didn't see "Adrien Brody's" load on your face. I don't know "Adrien Brody." I don't know who his girlfriend is either, but I picture her nail polish and wonder if she's my age and if she poured that nail polish onto her boyfriends balls and grinned as the lacquer dried.

What about him? Does he regret his actions? Does he feel like a slimy, arrogant douchebag? I wonder why he's off the hook and "Marie Calloway" is under the microscope. I also wonder why, as a woman interested in female subjectivity, she gave men exactly they wanted: a star-fucker, hipster chick with a load in her face. They would jerk off endlessly. Her father might too.

Maybe we shouldn't give them what they want all the time. Give them our beautiful legs open and lonesome. Let's give them furious, witty, enraged words and see if it tickles their fancy.

So, you've made some mistakes. We are not fucked. We are women who dig deep and write about our hideous parts with great love.

In my 20's and 30's I rooted out the women who saved my ass, and taught me craft. They are: Lorrie Moore, Mary Gaitskill, Michelle Tea, Eileen Myles, Cheryl Strayed, Lidia Yuknavitch, Dylan Landis, Susie Bright, Susan Straight, Sapphire, Mary Karr, Jeanette Winterson, Jennifer Egan, Dorothy Allison and Joan Didion.

Young writer, you are no Dave Eggers. You are no David Foster Wallace, writing to become "Unlonely." You are not "fucked" like the characters on the pages of a Tao Lin novel. You are a Daily Rumpus, an on-line journal story, a lovely little thing with an angelic face with moxie and nerve. You could be the girl on her back in thigh-high leg warmers on an American Apparel billboard. But, you're not. You're a writer. You've read some books. You've been an escort, and you've made a splash on the Internet by the age of 21. Writers I admire are bragging about you: Stephen Elliott, Roxane Gay, Tao Lin, and Alana Noel Voth.

Stephen Elliott was in my apartment once, handcuffed to a chair, hooded and blindfolded, penetrated by my cock. His head was lowered, almost touching his chest. I could hear him breathing. He seemed like who I wanted him to be. After red wax dripped down his spine, my friend Ronna arrived. She walked into my house with pictures and lightly mocked him, then left. I removed a red rag from his mouth. Know what I made him say?

"Tell me I'm a good writer." Like he had a choice.

"You're a good writer." His heart wasn't in it. I was crushed. He was a wet mouth, saying the words I wanted to hear

"I simply worry that if we continue to celebrate the Aderall-fueled, tit-flashing, brand-wearing that "Adrien Brody" exemplifies, we have less space for the truly remarkable literary labors of love. Wipe away the cum, and make some room for the glitter."

I don't dislike her because she writes openly about her sex life--I dislike her because she's just not very bright, and she seems to be cashing in on shock value to conceal that fact.

Would anyone have read anything Marie Calloway wrote, w[ould] she have secured this level of sad "microfame," if this wer[e] set up as the very easiest and most direct way for women to g[et] this level of attention? Re: reward v. punishment: the only worse sin than writing about sex is not writing about sex. This is a problem that predates her, that predates all young women who write about sex, that predates all young women who write, that predates all young women. It's a horrible systemic problem and let's unleash our rage upon it. Let's say that it's fucking terrible that the desire for attention, for women, is inevitably socially coded as a desire for sexual attention. It hurts women who engage and participate in becoming objects — and it also really hurts women who don't. Be horrified by her choices — they are bad choices. But also be horrified that it often looks like the only choice.

"This sounds really catty...but why does everyone keep referring to her as some "great beauty?" She doesn't really have any "it-factor"... she's just totally DTF."

As a female myself I find her annoying not because she's writing about sex or insecurities or popularity (yawn yawn yawn, that is what shitty-ass TV is for) but because she's kind of a moron. If she was intelligent, well-read, self-reflective, and had any non-selfish non-vapid ideas about anything I would like her. That is just what I like in people and

especially writers, gender aside.

"marie calloway is a lazy boring writer who i know through a friend to be histrionic, predictably 'unpredictable' and most likely autistic. WHO CARES."

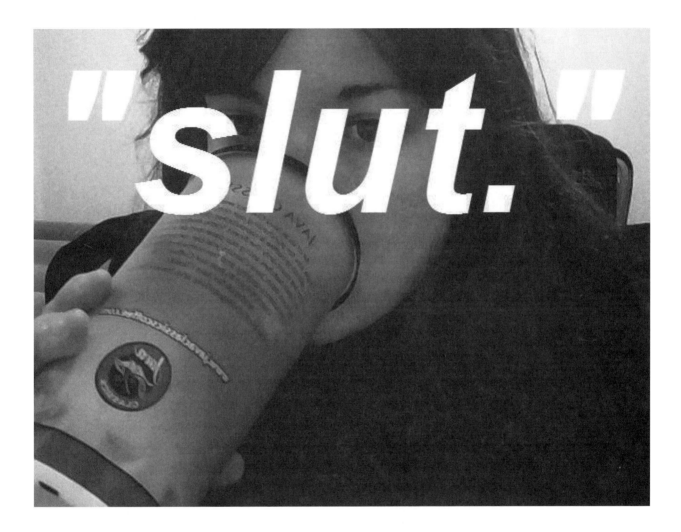

"And lastly, there's the fact that Marie Calloway makes me embarrassed and ashamed to be a female writer in my twenties."

jeremy lin

I emailed Jeremy Lin a story that I wrote at the behest of my friend. Not soon after, he emailed me back with this reply, "I liked it, if you make the capitalization normal and send it to me I'll publish it on the website of my publishing company, muumuuhouse.com." A few minutes later, he sent me a follow up email, "I got an idea. I'm going to France on December 3rd because they're translating my books. If you are in Paris from December 4 on 7:45AM until December 10 on 5:45PM, you can stay in my hotel room with me. But you have to 'cover' the entire trip, as if you are a journalist, in the style of all your other pieces, then get it published somewhere. (I'll help you find a venue). If I were rich I would pay for your plane ticket but I honestly have like $300 right now. But I am willing to pay half the amount of your plane ticket later, when the piece is published. I'll pay $700 of the ticket price after the piece is published. The piece should be at least 10,000 words."

I replied, "Okay, I edited the story so the capitalization is standard. I have attached it to the email. As for Paris, I'm interested but I might have trouble getting the funds. I'll keep you updated. Thank you very much for your interest in me and my writing of course. I feel very flattered."

"No problem. Sweet re: Paris. Sweet re: story. I will post it in one to seven days."

We emailed back and forth, fixing technical details in the story. Then he published it on the Muumuu House website. We arranged to chat on Gchat one afternoon about Paris.

"Hey. I feel like I was in a really social mood when I thought of the idea, now I feel like it'll be way too stressful," he typed.

"Okay. I probably couldn't get the money anyway."

*

A few days after Jeremy Lin published my story, I received an email from a reporter who wanted to do a phone interview with me about it.

"Hi Marie. I'm a reporter for the New York Observer. I'm writing because I read your story and admired it and want to write about it, and maybe first person writing/the Internet more broadly. I was wondering if I could interview you. What do you think?"

After thinking about it for days, I apprehensively agreed to do the interview with the encouragement and support of Jeremy Lin and my friends. The interviewer and I talked for an hour on the phone about my motivations and intentions with regards to writing, sexism in the literary world, Jeremy Lin, and aspects of writing on the Internet. The reporter ended the correspondence by saying that she would email interview Jeremy Lin for more information.

*

The day after the interview, Jeremy Lin forwarded me the responses he gave to the questions that he had received from the journalist.

"Tell me about how you met Marie Calloway. What did you think of her writing and also her as a person?'

"I've never met Marie in real life. Based on her Facebook, writing, Tumblr, etc., I think she's funny, kind, discerning, interesting, and attractively confident."

"'Why did you decide to publish her story on Muumuu House?'

"Simply because I liked it. I read it all at one time without stopping and was surprised, later, to learn it was ~15,000 words. It has similar qualities (detachment, focus, attention to certain funny/interesting details, lack of a "good/bad" agenda) of other writing I like that's autobiographical and first-person. (I'm thinking *The End of the Story* by Lydia Davis and *Good Morning, Midnight* by Jean Rhys), but maybe her writing is even more extreme and direct and even less sentimental."

I read this email several times in awe.

*

I felt anxious and uneasy the entire day before the piece came out. I had no idea what the article would say or how I would be represented in it. These feelings didn't subside after it was published; it was titled "Meet Marie Calloway: the New Model for Literary Seductress is Part Feminist, Part 'Famewhore' and All Pseudonyms" and the article itself was full of gossip ("compared to Ms. Calloway's other stories, *Adrien Brody* made bigger waves in literary New York because Mr. Brody was fairly well known here") rather than any focus on my story and "first person writing/the Internet" as I had been told it would. The reporter made a lot of conclusions and judgments about me and my writing that I didn't agree with ("with writing like Ms. Calloway's, it's tempting to believe that there is some sort of feminist impulse at work, that she derives power from humiliating men with her sexuality, the same tool they used to objectify her.") I felt uneasy to be suddenly upheld as a "feminist writer," which I had never thought of myself as and which seemed like a tremendous burden.

*

Jeremy Lin and I Gchatted about the article immediately after it was published on the web. He was also concerned about how he had been portrayed in the article. He quoted one of the mentions of him, "'The poet/novelist/deadpan literary provocateur [Jeremy] Lin, once rumored to be the author of Hipster Runoff, made a documentary about [Internet fashion model Bebe Zeva] early this year, in which Ms. Zeva, now 18, poignantly tells him about growing up without a father. Later, Mr. Lin sprays whipped cream on her face and rubs it in her hair'" and said, "I feel like I definitely come off as like I'm trying to prey on young girls and as an unseemly presence in the piece."

"Yes. I was concerned about that. I'm sorry that I helped to create a Jeremy Lin is a creep meme," I replied.

"I don't care. I feel like I feel nothing from any negative press about me anymore."

"Oh. Were you ever bothered?" I asked.

"I'm not really sure. I think since I didn't know anyone, and wouldn't be in contact with anyone who would have the opportunity to think bad things about me in real life, it just concretely had no effect on my life, which I was able to focus on. Now I feel like I always assume that I will probably like the person getting shit-talked and, based on experience, not to believe what's written. And I feel like the few people I'd be able to be friends with also think that way, so it doesn't affect me concretely. In terms of publicity, there was a study that showed that bad publicity helps more than good publicity, because it gets more attention. Then after like three years people forget if it was good or bad publicity, they just remember that you got publicity, which seems true.

"By the way, I feel like in the past I've felt really sensitive about pieces about me, like I viewed every single thing as negative, as you seem to be doing. For instance, when I read articles about me, other people would think what they were saying was good, but the same details about me I would think are bad. But I think that's just from being sensitive."

*

The day after the article came out, it was discussed on Gawker, a popular Internet gossip site, and HTMLGIANT, a popular literary site. There were hundreds of comments.

> "How is she going to feel when all her friends and family find out about her explicit blog about being a hooker in London. I am pro-sex and sex work and everything but this is not feminism, it's attention-whoring and it's going to blow up in her face when it's no longer cute." [female.]

> "I'm just offended that every teen who makes her diary public gets referred to as a "writer," as if sharing what are essentially Penthouse Forum-quality passages is some kind of challenging profession." [male.]

> "This is the literary equivalent of two straight girls making out on a keg in a field party. If this can be described as 'chronicles of women's sexuality,' so can Penthouse Letters. Anais Nin this ain't." [male.]

> "It bothers me that anyone would consider this scenario remotely compelling—a young girl desperate for attention and validation solicits a random, married writer twice her age in a position of relative authority for sex, he cums on her face (easily one of the most degrading sexual acts, and one heavily influenced by porn culture), she writes about it in awful prose that's borderline pornographic, and

you manage to find something redeemable from it all."
[male.]

"feminism as pure opportunism. let's fuck famous people and tell how shitty they are. or let's pretend to fuck famous people and tell. the younger we are the better. americans are such prudes. this whole deal would be so much more *edgy* if she were 15 or better yet 13. what's the legal limit? the sasha-grey-azation of society. It's my choice whether I profit off my documented degradation! if I profit, then I am in control! if I profit, I win! look at me! I can fuck famous people and hit buttons on a keyboard! I can take 10 cocks and then write about it! i'm a writer! joyce ain't got shit on me!" [sic] [male.]

"To write something like this pseudonymously in a fashion that outs the other person certainly meets the author's self-definition of 'fame whore' with the accent on the whore."
[male.]

"She's confused attention with power and has let herself be used, sexually and now by other writers who are more savvy than herself (who profits here?). Her sexual exploits seem to be traumatizing experiences that she orchestrates to tantalize people who get off on the degradation of women (including herself). She has written repeatedly about how she is frigid, how sex is painful to her and how violence turns her on because she was a victim of rape.
Just gross... and sad." [male.]

"marie calloway is a lazy boring writer who I know through a friend to be histrionic, predictably 'unpredictable' and most likely autistic." [sic] [female.]

I spent the entire day reading all that had been written about me. I incessantly ruminated over all of it to the point of mental exhaustion, working myself up to a panic attack which finally culminated in me hiding from my parent's Christmas party in the guest bathroom. There, I curled up into the fetal position and hyperventilated. After an hour and a half, I got up and logged onto my computer and went onto Gchat. Jeremy Lin immediately messaged me.

"How are you?" he asked.

"I don't know. Is it possible to pull my story off of Muumuu House?"

"I feel aversion to that but it's up to you."

"Yes. I don't know. I guess I should not decide while I'm panicking."

"I feel really good about all of this."

"Why?" I asked.

He sent me a long email titled, "why I feel good about all of this,"

"Benefits for Marie

1. More people know about you and writing, which makes you and your writing more valuable, which ensures you a larger chance of financial security. Financial security means that you will feel less pressure to do things that you don't want to do. Financial security also means that you will feel less pressure to compromise any of your views or art or writing or anything.

It also ensures you a larger number of people who know about you and view you as worthy of attention. This means you will have a wider range of people with which you can choose to talk to and be friends with. This means you will be less likely to 'settle' for someone in terms of friendship or romance; you have more of an ability to 'choose' who you like most. This is what I think when I get negative coverage or people say I'm an 'attention whore.' It's to ensure financial security, not to gain something called 'fame' which is an abstraction and so is something I have no concept of. I can't 'get' fame.

Benefits for People like Me

1. I'm excited about all this. I'm excited you exist. I feel less depressed because of this and your writing and you, in the same way I'm less depressed when I read any work of art that I like. This entire thing is so unlikely and exciting to me and in a way that is also positive, I feel, for society and everyone involved. As an 'art project' this is exciting to me. Something that I feel is morally good and artistically original/exciting is happening now and I feel less depressed or bored about life because of it."

"I'm glad that you are glad that I exist." I responded.

Jeremy Lin's email opened a floodgate inside of me, and I told Jeremy Lin all about my worries about writing, my feelings of alienation, as well as the guilt, humiliation, and anger ("We didn't talk about 'feminism' or 'famewhoring' or 'revenge' in the interview at all and I specifically asked the reporter not to focus on any gossip and she said she wouldn't. I was so stupid to not have known that would happen. I feel completely ashamed.") that I felt in a rapid fire stream-of-consciousness over Gchat. I concluded it with, "I feel like I will be embarrassed of this spill tomorrow. Please reassure me that you don't mind or think less of me."

"I enjoyed reading all that, thanks for sharing. There's nothing that you can say or do at this point that will make me think less of you, I feel. To me, I view this as: I'm happy to know someone like you, I have an increased chance of financial security (via increased knowledge of me), and that I'm happy to read your writing and see what happens with you and your writing in the future."

I then told him about my fears of what he had meant with the invitation to Paris, about how my friends and Internet commentators had said, and how even I had wondered, if that he was just trying to get me to have sex with him, and that that was the reason he had even published my story in the first place.

"No, I didn't want you to come to Paris to have sex. I like talking to you and I like your writing and your personality and sense of humor and willingness to publish things. I thought that I wanted to meet you and probably would at some point, and the most interesting way to do it would be to preempt you writing about it by making it the focus. I also knew that I wouldn't be able to do anything without consciousness of it being written about which seemed exciting, but only in a certain mood."

"I can't go into a situation knowing that I'll write about it," I responded.

*

After we were done chatting, I replayed the phrases "I'm excited that you exist" and "there's nothing that you can say or do at this point that will make me think less of you, I feel" over and over in my mind; it was successful in tampering the negative phrases that had been playing in my mind all day. No one had ever said anything like those things about me, and I realized that deep down it was what I was always longing to hear from other people, that all of my social interaction with other people was really just out of a want to hear those sentences, and so I felt almost existentially relieved by talking with him that night.

*

However, the intense criticism of me and my story on the Internet continued to grow. I began to receive death and rape threats over email. I mostly fought the compulsion to reply to the comments, and simply deleted the negative emails that I got. Nevertheless, a comment that essentially called me an "ugly slut" pushed me over the edge, and I broke my silence by responding "fuck off" to it. Right after I did that, I was immediately intensely embarrassed, but there was no way to delete my comment. I emailed Jeremy Lin out of desperation for consolation about everything.

"I am worried about how 'attention' makes me act weirdly. I tend to crack under pressure. I feel embarrassed about responding 'fuck off' to an idiotic comment on Thought Catalog. I feel like all of this 'attention' on the Internet is all very draining and exhausting, yet also addicting. I feel like it will be difficult for me to be able to write for a while due to reading all of these things about me, as stress and expectations on myself, and also the perceived expectations and opinions of others, make it impossible for me to write well. It seems like if I want to become a 'successful writer' it will be a lot harder than I imagined and in ways that I did not imagine. Maybe it won't even be possible due to how I crack under pressure. I just felt like telling you all this to get it out, by the way. I'm not expecting you to act as my therapist or something like that." I wrote.

"I feel like you already have enough for a book, so maybe you can relax for a while and focus on what you've already done. I feel like you navigated this as well as I can think. I feel glad to have been a part of this in some way. I feel like the most shit-talking you will ever receive has probably already happened, with this, and it will gradually decrease from now on, so there will be less stress maybe. Overall, just good job, thank you for sending the story to me in first place," Jeremy Lin replied.

"Thank you. I feel happy that I made you 'proud' of me, and that I helped you get hits."

*

After this message, Jeremy Lin and I Gchatted later that day.

"What do you think when someone says there are flaws in your writing, or when someone says you have talent? Do you think any of those people are right, whether they say you are good or bad, or do you think that everyone just has different preferences?" he asked.

"To be honest, I haven't really thought about it." I replied.

"If someone says your writing has flaws or is good, that implies they know a concrete goal that your writing has, which can be measured in numbers, and that the number would be higher or lower if you changed your writing in a certain way, I feel, but that seems incredibly hard to measure, even if two different people had agreed upon a purpose for your writing that could be measured, like 'increases heart rate in reader' or something. But it can be depressing to never think in terms of 'good'/'bad' without defining contexts/goals in each instance.

"I feel like it's two completely different ways of using language, to (1) never use abstractions with 100% seriousness especially qualitative ones, without defining contexts or goals. (2) To use them. (2) makes it so there's always some purpose, there's always some people who you view as having 'good taste' and others as 'bad taste' and there's always that 'conversation' happening, that argument. I think that like 98% of people are (2), but I can only do (2) self-consciously, because I know that it's not accurate. But out of all the people on the Internet, I've found some people who write things who do (1) mostly and have published them on Muumuu House."

I said that I appreciated his thoughts, but that I wasn't in a cerebral mood at that moment. In actuality, I was very interested in Jeremy Lin's opinion, but thought that I needed to do more reading and think on my own about this before I formed an opinion. But I was too afraid to tell him all of that.

*

A few days later, Jeremy Lin and I were invited to participate in a letter in the mail writing project, and also participate in a reading that was to be held in New York in connection with it. Jeremy Lin then arranged a Muumuu House reading to be held around that same time. He emailed me about the Muumuu House reading, "Would you want to confirm the reading for February 21?"

"Yes, the 21st it is. I just booked a plane ticket to New York today. I feel very grateful towards you."

"I'm excited that you're coming and that we have readings. I'm really glad that you're coming," he replied.

*

Until then, my interactions with Jeremy Lin had been overwhelmingly positive and supportive. Perhaps this led me to a false sense of complacency; that he would like me no matter what I did. Even with Jeremy Lin's emotional support, the onslaught of hundreds of comments calling me a horrible writer and attacking me personally got to me. Out of want for support, I emailed a writer that I admired. After I sent it to her, I forwarded the email to him, hoping that he would comfort me, even though the email contained these lines, "The 'attention' positive and negative is making me get into an unhealthy obsessive/self-hate cycle and I developed massive writer's block and I lost my voice and confidence in my ability to write. I know the thing to do is just to ignore all of the comments, but I can't help but read things about me. I hate how I'm being described as some Jeremy Lin imitator or groupie. I don't want to be really associated with Jeremy Lin/Muumuu House (as a writer), I really want to escape that shadow."

Jeremy Lin responded to the forward, "There will always be people talking about you if your writing is available. The more people who read your writing, the more money you'll make and the more people will talk about you. If you don't want any personal attention I think the only way to do that is to completely make up an identity and write only completely made up stories. Even if you have no Internet presence, if you publish a book, people will be talking about you. I think the only sustainable solution is to just learn over time to not be affected by what other people say or think. As for what you want or don't want to be associated with, focus on what you like and publish your work at places you like, and talk to people you like, and that's what you'll be associated with and if it's what you like then that won't be a problem. But being associated with things is unavoidable also."

I could tell that he was upset with me. I wrote him a reply email, "I'm sorry if I came off as rude or offensive with regards to what I said about not wanting to be associated with you or Muumuu House. I didn't mean it like that, I don't know. I really feel very grateful to you for publishing me on Muumuu House, and all of the advice and support that you have given me."

Jeremy Lin replied, "Can you elaborate on 'I didn't mean it like that, I don't know' as much as you can or want to? I feel that it would decrease the awkwardness I feel now, and also I'm interested. I'm also interested in any elaboration of your original email. I would like to know more. Who do you seek validation from? From reading your blog and Facebook, I feel like you place more value in writing that is political and uses academic terms, but your fiction is nothing like that. I think it's interesting, the difference. I can see how you wouldn't want to be associated with certain things. I am interested in hearing more, both out of interest and to decrease the awkwardness."

"I'm sorry. I don't want things to be awkward. I don't want you to dislike me or think less of me. I'm not sure who I seek validation from. I feel like I would be unhappy and insecure unless every single person who read my writing said they liked it and got what I was intending to do 100% and obviously that is impossible. I think deep down I published things because there was a desire to be understood by other people, but that didn't really happen and it now seems kind of ridiculous to think that could happen. Instead there were just a lot of people misunderstanding me and totally misrepresenting me as a stupid Jeremy Lin puppet attention whore.

"I guess those people don't matter but it was very frustrating. Why do other people feel they understand my motivations and intentions with regards to my writing? Why do they feel like they can write in detail about my mental health? Why do they feel they get to decide if I'm 'degrading' myself, and assume that I have no understanding of those things? Why do they get to decide that just because my writing seems straightforward and direct, or that because I'm a 21-year-old 'girl' that I can't have any intent with regards to my writing that isn't directly stated? And so on... I guess I just feel like I don't want to be associated with you as a writer in the way that it brings people to think my whole writing efforts are just to impress you/get famous/attempt to write exactly like you.

"As a writer and as a person I admire and like you a lot. I like how you are very intelligent but don't feel the need to show it off and are completely sincere and unpretentious, and I feel the same about your writing. Probably I was trying to use publishing as a way to bypass forming real life relationships with people, which is very difficult for me to do via awkwardness and social anxiety. I also feel like I desired to be validated by people as a writer and wanted to be able to see myself as a writer. I realized that I do want a book though I know I won't make much money or probably be reviewed well. I can't say why really that I write. I don't really aim to make money so much as like you said you did (not that I think wanting to make money is a bad goal). Writing is just something that I've done everyday since I was like seven years old and it feels like something I have to do, the same as with eating or whatever, but I feel like I come off as pretentious or taking myself really seriously if I say that. I don't want to be pretentious or ambitious and I really dislike those qualities in other people. I hate any sort of artifice. I feel like I can see myself becoming someone who is very ambitious and careerist and tries to suck up to people and who brags about being published in places, and I don't want to be like that, and I can't really operate or write under those conditions," I responded.

"Thanks for typing all of that, I feel less awkward. Some people understood you and your writing. Wanting to connect with people is also a main factor as to why I write and publish things, forgot to mention that. Don't you feel you were successful in that? You've met a lot of people through writing. You didn't feel ambitious before? What were you thinking when you were sending out stories and emailing me a lot of times even if I didn't respond, with your writing? Is it different now? I'm interested in what you think about Muumuu House, because I honestly feel that Muumuu House is the least careerist, sucking up, 'contest'-like thing for writing there is now that I know of, since I and most people published that I know of on the site honestly believe that there is no good or bad in art (for example I 100% believe a 10-year-old's writing is not less good than James Joyce's, or replace either with any people) and have demeanors where it's impossible to fake interest or 'suck up.' I feel like someone who wants to avoid those things you listed would feel an affinity with Muumuu House. But I also think that you want validation and it's an environment where you won't get much. I don't value intelligence and feel aversion to the word 'talent.' I feel like based on your stories I would think that you would like my writing, but based on other aspects of you I feel like you wouldn't like my writing. I feel like if there is anything I'm the opposite of it's probably essays I've read by *n+1* people. So I've felt vague about what you think about me and why you repeatedly send me things. Can you elaborate on that? Also, what do you think about all the advice people have given you? I've felt aversion whenever I've read any advice people have given you. I feel like you know what you're doing and when I read other people's advice it makes me feel like I want to help you feel like you don't need their advice," Jeremy Lin wrote.

"It's true that some people understood my writing, and my friends who knew me well grew to understand me more. For instance, my friend said, 'my girl friend in high school really likes your writing and admires you. I think there are a lot of people, girls especially, who intuitively understand what you're writing about and feel excited about it.' I guess it's hard for me to focus on that, though. It's also true that I started to talk to a lot of people I really like because of my writing. I guess it just comes back to insecurity; a desire to be recognized by intellectuals or everyone, even. I don't know what to do about that. I don't know why I sent you things. I feel like I was just on autopilot and did those things because they intuitively felt like the thing to do and there wasn't conscious thought behind it. I didn't know or think much at all about Muumuu House before, and I had never read any of the writers there except I read a few of your short stories and *Richard Yates,* but I read those way after I published writing on Thought Catalog and sent you writing. I see some competition, ambition, and sucking up though it is in a different way than in other places.

"I admire how firmly you feel about all art being subjective. I don't know how I feel about it. I haven't thought or read enough about it, though my intuitive feeling is that it isn't, totally, but now I'm thinking more and more that all art is subjective, but again, I don't feel like I've read or thought about it enough to have a legitimate opinion. The most cynical part of me feels like it is a cop-out, with regards to my own writing, if I were to believe that all art is subjective. I haven't really thought about or read about 'talent', though I can imagine that it is similar.

"As for you with regards to your writing, I liked *Richard Yates,* and a few weeks ago I bought *Shoplifting from American Apparel.* Before you published my stories, my interest in you was sort of 'sociological'; I was more interested in you as a sort of cultural entity than as a writer or person and I read *Richard Yates* through this lens, as well as the idea that I acquired of you (without thinking on my own) that you were just a talentless, gimmicky writer. Now, it's different, of course. I think, partly, that sending things to you was just kind of a social experiment. I was curious as to how you would react. I never expected you to publish anything by me.

"About liking and admiring academic and intellectual writing but my own fiction not being like that, I feel like I'm fascinated by that kind of writing and I think it's more interesting than fiction. I think a lot about politics, but I'm not confident enough to write about those sorts of things directly, only indirectly through fiction. Maybe I'm not intelligent enough, either. It's really frustrating to be someone who is genuinely interested in things, but perhaps lacks the intelligence to directly contribute to any sort of meaningful intellectual discourse. Also, the way that I think is not so rationally, but often intuitively and emotionally, and I make 'high ideas' cognizant mostly through the lens of myself and my personal experiences. Obviously this doesn't work for that kind of academic writing," I wrote.

"Why do you think that thinking your writing is subjective and is a cop-out? It makes life even harder for you (because you won't be with the 95% or whatever that believe otherwise) and (I've written about this elsewhere but don't know where exactly, just trust me that I've thought about it a lot) it's moral, it reduces pain and suffering in the world, to view art as subjective (basically it reduces hierarchical thinking and reduces qualitative-abstraction thinking; outside of morals it's historically, I estimate, more original; finally, it's more accurate, going by natural laws). In terms of how much you work on your writing, art being subjective or not is irrelevant. Everyone still has their ideals if art is subjective and it will take as much work for someone to make a story into their ideal if they believe art is subjective or not.

I'd be much more interested in reading political or other essays by you than something via *n+1*, something with a lot of terms and received ideas. I feel like, based on what I know, a larger percentage of advances in whatever field have come from non-academic people who were able to think concretely and without the use of terms (or something). In your fiction you're able to write how things are, I feel, not how one would think they are, having read thousands of novels. I feel like you have a brain that is able to view things without preconceptions, in terms of your fiction, but you are resisting using that for other things. That you were really seeking validation is what I sensed whenever you asked me for help or advice."

After this conversation I thought about how I admired Jeremy Lin's obvious intelligence and thoughtfulness, though I wondered if he was trying to mold my thoughts and ideas and felt uncomfortable.

*

The rest of the week leading up to the readings in New York, Jeremy Lin continued to at times emotionally support me and give me advice on publishing my writing over email, and I felt touched when he expressed concerns about his own writing to me. He mailed me a booklet of drawings of koalas clutching onto cats that he drew for me, and I looked at it often.

*

I arrived in New York City on February 17. I was staying at an Internet acquaintance's house, and the night culminated in me coercing him into holding me while I cried and shook from the immense anxiety I felt about being in New York to meet Jeremy Lin and to do readings, an anxiety which I summed up to him in one line, "I just feel like I owe everyone something, and I can't deliver."

"They like you because of the work you produced. You don't need to offer anyone more than that. You don't owe anyone anything. Look, even if Jeremy and all of those people hate you in real life, which won't happen, you don't need them. You don't need any of those people," the acquaintance said.

Laying there I thought: I know that I don't "need" Jeremy Lin to be a writer, but that's not what I'm concerned with. Or perhaps I do need Jeremy Lin, because I know that without his emotional and public support I would have cracked. I want Jeremy Lin to like me a lot, though I don't know how much I genuinely like him as a person and how much my feelings are distorted by him being Jeremy Lin. I then thought about how I couldn't explain to anyone how I feel that my entire social existence amounts to a burden for other people, about how guilty I feel for making them interact with me, and how I know that the only hope for anyone to enjoy interacting with me is if I'm somehow able to conceal my real personality.

*

On Friday, I emailed Jeremy Lin asking if he wanted to meet me on Saturday. He said that he couldn't, but that we should meet the day of the reading, a few hours before the event. On that day, we arranged to meet at a smoothie shop called One Lucky Duck. I took a taxi there and stood outside of it, smoking. I had to wait a while because I had arrived about twenty minutes early. I had been very afraid of being late as I had gleaned from his books that Jeremy Lin hated lateness.

After waiting about half an hour, I saw Jeremy Lin walking towards me, carrying a MacBook. He was smiling. I started to smile when I saw him, and I wondered if it was because I was happy to see him, or if I was happy because he was smiling when he saw me.

We said hello to each other. Inside, Jeremy Lin helped me pick out a smoothie and bought it for me.

We sat side by side in a booth.

"Is that a tattoo?" Jeremy Lin asked of the name TOM written on my arm in black sharpie.

"No. It's the name of my best friend. I wrote it today so that I would feel less nervous."

Jeremy Lin nodded. We sat in silence for a few moments.

"I liked it when Adrien Brody said 'Am Appy' in your story."

"Yeah, that was funny."

Jeremy Lin gave me Xanax so that I would feel less nervous during the reading, and we split a tablet of MDMA. He put it directly into my mouth with his fingers. I thought about how people on the Internet would write about Jeremy Lin "drugging young girls" if they knew about this.

He turned to look at my face and sighed, "I can't believe I'm twenty-eight."

He started to tap on random keys at a rapid-fire pace on his MacBook. "I'm typing the URL to my secret blog," he said. I laughed.

He wasn't talking, just hitting random keys on his MacBook out of what seemed to me like boredom.

"Am I doing something wrong?" I asked.

"No. I feel like I can talk to you."

He asked me what I had been doing in New York so far.

"Yesterday I met with the guy who wrote the shit-talking post about me that you responded to. He said he's going to come to the reading, but he doesn't know why because he hates Muumuu House. He hates *n+1* too, though."

"I feel like there's people who like Muumuu House, then there's people who like *n+1*, and then there's those other people."

"Yeah. I thought that people usually like one or the other. He was really nice and seemed really smart, though. I think I have a crush on him."

"I don't get crushes anymore," Jeremy Lin said.

This seemed sudden, and kind of severe to me. I felt a little taken aback. We sat in silence for a while.

"I feel like you don't like me," I said finally.

"No, I like you, I like you, I definitely like you."

I pinched his arm with my index and middle finger. His arm felt tiny and bony and I didn't like the feel of it.

"What are you doing?" he asked, and I stopped. This was my blatant attempt at flirting, and it had failed. I said that I was sorry and felt buzzed from the Xanax.

Then I said that I was attracted to him. I wasn't sure if I was attracted to him or not, but said that I was because I was confused as to how he felt towards me and wanted to know.

"In what way are you attracted to me?" he asked.

"Isn't there only one way to be attracted to someone?"

"Like you would have sex with me?"

"Yeah."

"Who *wouldn't* you have sex with?"

I felt offended by this, but just smiled and said, "Frat boys at my school who hit on me."

"That's…" he said, brushing me off.

"I thought you only liked really tall guys," he said.

"I care mostly about age and intelligence, I guess."

He said that he thought that before we met that I had made a point of saying that I wasn't attracted to him.

"I just said that because I didn't want to make you uncomfortable."

"You are attractive…I'm just not attracted to anyone. I watch too much porn," he said, smiling.

"I'm sorry. I feel kind of affected by the Xanax. This is a really awkward conversation."

He said that it was fine, and that he liked awkward conversations.

*

He said that he had to meet his friend at a bar, and so we left and started to walk towards it.

He began to talk about the email that I had forwarded to him.

"You are so smart and like, confident in your writing. I want to make you feel like you don't need those people's advice. Like I feel like there's like fifteen versions of some writers, but…" I guessed the implication was that there was only one Marie Calloway. I was flattered, but I also thought about how he was urging me not to listen to anyone's advice, while at the same time he frequently gave me advice. I wondered if what he really wanted was for me to only listen to his advice.

He asked me exactly what I had meant about what I had said in the forward about him and Muumuu House.

"I feel like I already told you, in that email I sent to you."

I felt confused and frustrated by his disbelief and lack of satisfaction in my explanation, and wondered if perhaps that this was the result of there being something about the way that female writers are treated that male writers can't grasp.

"I just feel like there's something you're not telling me," he said.

"I feel like there's something you're not telling *me*," I said, wondering about why he was badgering me about this issue after I had explained it to him the best that I could.

"It makes me feel like you're using me to further your writing career."

"No!" I said, and stopped in the middle of the street, my arm stretched out towards him. I was completely shocked that he thought that.

"What are you doing?" he asked, laughing.

I walked to the sidewalk where he was standing, and he started to walk again, but then I stopped and started to rub my eyes, halfway in between actually crying and forcing myself to cry. I wanted to cry so he would see that I was a good person and not a calculating user, but he seemed completely unfazed by my tears. He discussed people using other people in the literary world, and how most people had relationships like that, and about how it was okay to be honest and acknowledge them.

"I feel like you're projecting qualities of other people or yourself onto me," I said. I didn't really think that, but I couldn't think of any other way to articulate that I thought that he was wrong.

"I don't think I am," he said, smiling and shaking his head.

I thought then how it seemed impossible for me or perhaps even anyone to outsmart or manipulate Jeremy Lin, at least when it came to interacting with him on an interpersonal level.

"Can we start walking again?" I asked.

"Yeah. You were the one who stopped."

We began to walk again and were silent for a while until Jeremy Lin said, "You didn't get *Good Morning, Midnight*, did you?!" in a playfully accusatory tone.

"No, I got it," I insisted, and felt relieved that he had dropped the issue of the email, though also sad about how he seemed to believe that I was indeed only trying to use him.

"But you didn't start reading it yet?" he asked.

"I started it but, I don't know. I like writers like Raymond Carver and Tolstoy and Joyce Maynard."

"I feel like Jean Rhys is a lot more similar to how you write than how Raymond Carver or Tolstoy write. Are you not interested in reading writers who are similar to you?"

"I don't know."

*

We reached the bar and Jeremy Lin and I met his friend, a writer who would also be reading that night. They talked about drugs, facing each other with their backs to me. I sat staring ahead at the bartender. I ordered a beer and drank it rapidly, feeling suddenly very alone. I thought about what a quiet, ignorable presence I had. I wondered if for as long as I was with Jeremy Lin and there were other people there, I would always feel like a hanger-on.

*

Jeremy Lin, I, and the other writer walked into St. Mark's Bookshop together. There were about eighty people crowded inside. I felt simultaneously excited and high on a sense of "celebrity," and yet intensely ridiculous for feeling that way, as well as anxious. This was to be my first reading.

We all separated and I talked to the friends who had come to see me read as well as to a few fans of my writing who approached me.

After about half of an hour of talking and waiting, Jeremy Lin came to the microphone and announced that the reading was going to begin. I was sitting in the very front in a row of seats that had been reserved for all of the readers.

Jeremy Lin opened the reading and introduced himself. He read from his Twitter feed ("horror movie titled 'Flying Shark that can Open Locked

Doors'") and after reading thirty or so tweets ended abruptly by saying, "that's all I'm going to read," and introduced me. The crowd applauded. I walked to the microphone.

"Thank you very much. I'm Marie. I'm going to be reading from a story that I wrote called 'Adrien Brody' …" I continued to awkwardly explain my story. I felt strange, but I had thought before how I should explain it, because otherwise I would come off as arrogant, a sort of unspoken "*of course* you've heard of me and my story." Through the corner of my eye I saw Jeremy Lin smiling as I was explaining, like he was embarrassed, embarrassed of me.

"I'm sorry, I'm really nervous," I said, laughing, as an apology to Jeremy Lin.

I began to read. I kept my eyes firmly on the paper and was able to become unaware that there was a crowded bookstore full of people watching me. While I read I felt like I was able to become like an automaton. I recited the words on the page without thinking or feeling much. But near the end of my reading, someone laughed after I read the line "I could feel him lose his erection," breaking the audience's silence. After the laugh, I looked up from the paper I was reading from at the audience. I was terrified by the sight of a hundred blank faces, staring. I quickly looked back at the paper and (shakily at first) began to read again.

When I was done reading everyone applauded and I walked back to my chair and hung my head down, with my face in my hands. I thought I had done well, but that I should present myself as being ashamed so that others would judge me less.

*

After the reading, Jeremy Lin and the rest of the Muumuu House readers went to Blue and Gold, a nearby bar, along with all of their friends. While I was talking to my friend, Jeremy Lin came up behind me and placed his hand on my shoulder. I thought about how I liked the feeling of his hand on my shoulder.

"How are you feeling?" he asked.

"I feel like I didn't do well." I did actually think that I had done well, or at least okay, but I wanted him to say something nice about me.

"You did a good job," he said.

We didn't talk the rest of the night. Jeremy Lin talked to his other writer friends, and I talked to my friends who had come to see me read. But at the end of the night, I hugged Jeremy Lin before he left. As I embraced him, I felt like he hadn't wanted me to hug him and felt uncomfortable. He felt very thin, even skeletal, to hug.

I was left thinking that he hadn't liked me.

*

The next day Jeremy Lin emailed me, "How's it going, how was your day? What'd you do?"

"Hi. In the morning I took the train from this guy's house to back home. Then I went to meet this literary agent. He was very kind and seems to really like me and seems interested in representing me, I think, maybe, but says my next move is to get published in places like Harper's before releasing a short story collection. That's what people want first, apparently. After that I slept a lot. I feel lonely yet sick of people."

"I'm interested in hearing about you and the agent. I feel like there would be an agent who would want to sell a book by you now, if you put a book together out of the things you have and maybe one more thing first then approached them with that. I don't think Harper's, etc. is necessary. I feel like it's nearly impossible to get published in Harper's unless you have major connections but you can get a book published without connections."

"I'll think about all of those things and ask people about it. Do you want to hang out today? I'm meeting this guy for lunch today at 1:30 and then I'm free until the reading," I replied.

"You can ask me about book things. I feel like I know what I'm talking about re: agents and books. I'm meeting someone at 6:30 or so but I want to hang out with you. I'll be done with the library at 4:30. I'm at 79 Washington Sq. South or I can meet you wherever. I'll have email or text until then. I can give you some Xanax if you want."

*

I took the R train to 8th street and we met outside of the station. Jeremy Lin examined my copy of "Monthly Review," and then he led me to a vegan restaurant because I said that I wanted a drink before the reading.

When we arrived, I sat down and ordered a 32-ounce Sierra Nevada.

"How was meeting with the agent?" he asked.

"I think he liked me a lot."

"Why? Why would anyone like *you*?" he asked in a jocular tone.

"I don't know," I said, laughing.

He must like me, you would only joke like that with someone you really like, I thought.

We started to discuss the reading. He read the last line of the piece he was going to be reading that night ("when I read my mom's e-mail I cried also") and asked me if I thought that he should add other reasons that he had started to cry then, like how he had no friends at the time.

"I think that's kind of a cop-out," I said.

"It's more honest."

In the end he decided to read it as it was originally written.

*

We started to walk to Housing Works Books, where the reading was being held.

"Who do you think is the biggest fan of your writing?" Jeremy Lin asked.

I smiled. "I don't know. Probably no one."

"It's me."

*

When we arrived at the reading, Jeremy Lin separated from me to be with his friend, who was thin and pretty and blonde. I sat in the seats reserved for readers, and spent most of my time watching Jeremy Lin chatting, huddled up with the blonde woman, looking at his iPhone together. The first reader read, and then it was my turn to read. I got on the stage and read like an automaton again. When I was finished, the audience applauded me, and then I returned to my seat. I didn't pay attention to any of the readers. I only looked at Jeremy Lin talking with the blonde woman.

*

After the reading was finished I went over to Jeremy Lin and stood next to him. As we were talking, he was approached by a large group of fans. I stood there awkwardly as Jeremy Lin turned towards the group and began to talk with different people.

As I stood there looking at Jeremy Lin and his crowd I thought about how I desired to be close to him, for him to like me above all, and yet also how I felt overshadowed and stifled by him. Here, literally, as audience members flocked to him and everyone ignored me, and also as a writer, as my most honest thoughts and experiences were summed up by many as a Jeremy Lin imitation; a gushing groupie's love letter to an older writer she desperately wanted to be fucked by. I thought back to a comment about me that I had read: "a story by a young, immature writer who's trying to impress her writing idol [Jeremy Lin]" and how I would probably always feel stifled and overshadowed unless I were to somehow totally disavowal Jeremy Lin from my life and career, and accept all of the difficulty and pain that would bring. I wondered if I would ever be able to reconcile my ambition to be a serious writer with my desire to be loved.

*

At the end of the reading, Jeremy Lin, the blonde woman, my friend who had come to the reading, and I decided to go to Jeremy Lin's apartment. There wasn't enough room in the cab for all of us, so Jeremy Lin told my friend and I to take another cab and meet them. When we arrived on Jeremy Lin's street, he hadn't been waiting for us. I thought of a documentary I had once watched featuring an interview with Cynthia Lennon where she talked about being left behind by John Lennon on a train and how she knew then that their relationship was over. Then I felt ridiculous. I texted Jeremy Lin for his exact address.

*

My friend and I arrived at Jeremy Lin's apartment. He and four other people were there. While walking in, I was struck by the starkness of it. It was dimly lit, and was totally bare except for a bed and other necessities.

I went to Jeremy Lin's desk and took two tablets of MDMA, and an Adderall.

I went over to Jeremy Lin.

"Can I smoke in your room?" I asked.

"No, no no no…"

I smoked outside of the window, along with the four other people there. The blonde woman who Jeremy Lin had been conversing with at the reading tried to talk to me. She said kind things to me while I thought mean things about her.

I went onto Jeremy Lin's bed, where his MacBook was lying, with his Gmail open. I typed "Marie" into the search bar. I clicked on an email conversation that he had with another writer who had read at the Muumuu House reading.

"I like Marie in person, but I'm not attracted to her," Jeremy Lin had written.

"I expected to be more attracted to Marie in person. Also, I felt Marie read 'poorly', but she has a good reading voice," the writer had replied.

I stopped reading.

"What did he mean by that?" I asked to Jeremy Lin who had come to sit next to me on the bed.

"It's in quotes. You know what it means."

"Like it was *conventionally* a poor reading?"

"Yes, that's what it means."

I felt like I was acting like what men refer to as "difficult and needy," but on drugs I couldn't restrain myself.

"Why aren't you attracted to me?" I asked.

"I'm only attracted to girls who weigh like 100 pounds."

"You think that I'm using you, like a sociopath," I said.

"No."

Jeremy Lin moved away to talk to the other people in the room.

I got onto his MacBook and Google searched "Marie Calloway" and intentionally sought out negative things that had been written about me. ("It was just a girl mimicking [Jeremy Lin.]")

Jeremy Lin saw what I was looking at and scoffed. He ordered me to stop looking at those things because "it's just going to make you sad."

"Don't you think there's more things in life than just being happy? But, no, actually I feel silly that I cared so much about criticisms of me. It seems so immaterial in the face of doing readings and meeting with an agent and being surrounded by encouraging people…"

"Good."

I got off of the computer and talked to my friend, who was standing near the window. We talked about men and body image and writing.

"I remember that you said that one day you want to write a story that's completely incomprehensible to men," my friend said.

"Yeah, I do," I said, smiling.

"That's sexist. You're the most sexist person I've ever met," Jeremy Lin interjected.

I flopped down on his bed, sighing, "Men are so oppressed."

"Me and my friend were talking about how it seems ridiculous to call you a 'feminist,' but you support a lot of female writers through Muumuu House and you wrote that article about how female writers are taken less seriously than male ones."

"I did write that… I think everyone is sexist and racist."

I lit a cigarette and started to smoke it in Jeremy Lin's bed.

I said something to Jeremy Lin about inconsiderateness.

"How am I inconsiderate?"

"In your books," I said, thinking in my mind how a review in the New York *Times* had referred to the Jeremy Lin character in one of his books, *Richard Yates*, as a "psychologically damaging bully." I thought about how calling him a "bully" was too harsh, but that he had seemed really controlling and intent on molding the female character in that book, and that this was interesting to me because I thought that he had been trying to mold me as well.

He was going to respond, but then I sat up, revealing cigarette ash all over his white sheets.

"This was incredibly inconsiderate!" This was the first time I had ever heard, even heard of, Jeremy Lin raising his voice.

"Well, now you'll always have a part of me in your bed," I said, smiling and laughing.

He looked me and I averted his gaze. I could tell he was disgusted.

"I need to write," I said.

"What do you need to write?"

I didn't know. I didn't have anything in mind, I just felt that I had to, in that moment. Jeremy Lin slid his MacBook to me and looked over my shoulder. I typed about how I felt that Jeremy Lin owed me something, that he had a responsibility to me.

"I feel like I have given you a lot of publicity," he typed back.

I felt annoyed that he seemed to not understand what I had meant.

I typed bad things that had happened to me in my life, and that how I thought that usually male writers wrote female characters poorly, but that his portrayal of a teenage girl in *Richard Yates* was exceptional.

Jeremy Lin got up off of the bed and walked away to talk with his other friends.

My friend and I lay on Jeremy Lin's bed and talked intimately. Then Jeremy Lin addressed me, standing up, holding a copy of his book, *Bed*.

"I didn't like that one. I liked *Richard Yates*, though," I said.

"You don't like pretentious prose?" he asked, smiling.

I asked him if he would give me a copy of *Selected Unpublished Blog Posts of a Mexican Panda Express Employee* because I had enjoyed the author's reading.

"Won't that book just make you jealous?"

"*Why* would it make me jealous?"

"You know, she is my wife."

"I know."

He threw four or five Muumuu House books at my head.

*

The other guests at the party decided that it was time to leave, and left. Jeremy Lin and my friend urged me to leave as well, but I said that I didn't want to yet, and that I would catch up with my friend in a few minutes.

Jeremy Lin was lying stretched out on the other side of his bed, as far away from where I was sitting on it as possible. I said things, and he didn't respond.

Finally he said, "Your friend is waiting for you," with a high degree of irritation in his voice.

I thought about how normally being some place and interacting with someone when they don't want me to, as Jeremy obviously didn't then, is one of my worst fears. However, while I was on drugs I didn't care about any of that. I thought that it was interesting how I was for the first time in my life pushing past the desire to never interact with someone in a way that they didn't want me to.

"Oh, yeah." I had genuinely forgotten about her. I realized that I should leave for her sake.

"I just don't want you to lose interest in me and stop talking to me, Jeremy," I said quietly.

He said no, and that he only publishes people on Muumuu House that he thinks he will be interested in for a long time.

I got out of his bed and walked out of his apartment.

*

When I got back home from New York, the first thing that I did was email Jeremy Lin.

"Hi. I'm sorry if I made you uncomfortable at the party thing. It's just drugs make me spill my guts. I feel like you would be interested in that in my fiction but not from the high, crazy girl at a party. I'm not sad you aren't attracted to me, really, by the way."

"It's okay. I usually like talking in that manner, just not at that moment. I had also felt irritated by your other actions, like how you got cigarette ash everywhere. So I didn't feel like talking like that at that moment. But I liked talking to you at other times. Did I give you *you are a little bit happier than I am*? Almost all of it is about a girl I liked that I wanted to be closer to who didn't want to be closer to me. I feel like I felt how you felt when you were lying in the bed not wanting to leave. It's in one of the poems in there, where I don't want to leave some girl's place but she's kicking me out."

I wanted to ask why he had told me about that part in his book, but I was too afraid to.

*

"I don't think Jeremy Lin likes me anymore. I'm afraid that he's lost interest in me," I wrote in an email to a mutual friend of Jeremy Lin and I.

A few minutes after I sent that email the friend responded, "I don't think you understand him. You expect him to see you as a sex object, but he sees you as a person, and as a writer. You should stop thinking of sex as your best thing and realize, like Jeremy has, that writing is your best thing."

insufferable

May 4

did you know that i saved some of your more risqué photos from your Facebook a long time ago and looked at them before bed sometimes

"can you just be mine and mine only from now on?"

marie

k

u can get drunk and act lovey dovey to me

Z

was not an act

Z

i am in love

Z

i think i told ppl at the party that i am in love w marie calloway

marie

yay

Z

'why isnt she here'

Z

did you get yr itinerary at kahimikarie@yahoo?

Marie Calloway

yes

:)

Marie Calloway

ri 25MAY

LV 2:00pm LAS VEGAS
AR 8:58pm
DETROIT

Z

i am really happy for the first time in a few weeks

Marie Calloway

me too

marie

hm

hope if i break your heart u make intensely misogynistic but amazing piece of art about me

z

duh

the art will just be a collage of a bunch of pictures of my dick juxtaposed with chicken wings

titled, "lick it clean, marie calloway you piece of shit."

marie

k

z

i want to fall asleep tonight and then wake up in a car on the way to pick you up from the airport

marie

yes

http://i50.tinypic.com/517yns.jpg my last friday before i'm married/pregnant. i'm hideous! (✿'◡'✿)

"I feel like I belong here."

"it's scary how much you look like anna karina. it's scary how beautiful you are. you are going to destroy me."

am i always going to feel like this? uncomfortable, tired, bored, irritable, depressed.

"i feel exhausted."

"[being around you makes me feel depressed.]"

"how is marie?"

"insufferable."

"it's like she has never interacted with another human being, ever."

"she's so weird and boring. i don't know how much longer i can take being around her."

"Baby."

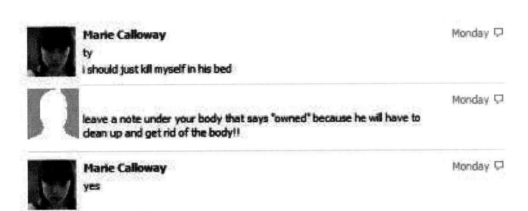

Marie Calloway   Monday ⤶
ty
i should just kill myself in his bed

                                                      Monday ⤶
leave a note under your body that says "owned" because he will have to
clean up and get rid of the body!!

Marie Calloway   Monday ⤶
yes

"i feel like a monster. last night you kept telling me to 'stop', and i didn't."

"we were just playing."

actually, trying to push him off of me was one of the most erotic and pleasurable experiences of my life.

Hey buddy, was asked to email you by Marie. Hope it doesn't make things too much weirder.

Anyway, I'm not messaging you to tick you off or anything, simply to try and explain her a little. She is, as I'm sure you've discovered by now, quite a tough nut to crack. She is way more scared and introverted than her online persona may suggest. There are lots of reasons for this we won't go into, but the upshot is that she really isn't like other girls.

She really can't deal being around lots of people, or even a few. That's a lesson I learned after many long hard struggles myself; eventually I learned that no matter how much you want her to meet your friends, she can't. She simply isn't able to get her like that. People scare her at the best of times. She could only do the book readings in NYC on a buttload of MDMA for instance, and even then she was panicking.

The other thing you need to know is that she cannot take criticism. It locks her up. She gets scared.

Basically, she needs to be treated with inhuman patience. That's hard for people to do, I think, and hard for them to grasp. Right now, she feels disliked and burdensome, which I am perfectly sure you didn't mean to do. Life's been cruel enough to her, though, that she feels this sort of thing after even mild criticism even when it's not meant. It sucks, but that's the situation.

As guillermo suggests, a bit of beer might loosen her up and relax her, because right now she's wound up tight and very scared. It's solvable, with great patience, maybe some hugs if she'll let you. She may or may not be able to talk about it, but she's not very emotionally articulate when you have her in front of you.

Not sure what else to say. Sorry top dump unsolicited advice on you. I'll understand if it makes you cross for me sending you this - it's a weird-ass situation. I'm just worried about my friend. For what it's worth, I don't think for a minute you've been cruel or mean to her. It's just a case of your being quite unprepared for the crazy world of Marie Calloway. If you need more tips on dealing with her, do ask. I genuinely do understand her up to a point, after long years of hard learning

I feel humiliated

"i told her i liked her."

…
"i guess i just wanted to see how you'd react."
he's mean to me for fun.
["I do actually like you a lot … I'm afraid of my feelings for you …. I'm like a little boy who teases a girl he likes."]
he doesn't feel that way at all. he's just trying to manipulate me. over the internet i became interested in him because he talked about being manipulative. he seemed very intelligent.

someone told me to hit them and i hit them and it felt good. and then i strangled them. i told my mom i think i am misogynistic maybe because i like being mean to women sometimes	10:35 PM
i feel like i manipulate a lot of people. i have never felt like a situation was out of my control, and if i have, i didn't care.	10:36 PM

i felt a connection to him, i wanted to be around him.

Marie Calloway
Monday

"i hate you."

Like · Comment

👍 Akiko Yoshida, Christa Harader and 5 others like this.

"I want to be close to you."
"we are close. we're laying on a twin mattress together."
"You know what I mean. Why will you feel 'relieved' when I go home on Friday?"
"We've already had this conversation."
am i not even worth talking to?

marie
sweet marie

mew
sweet
i miss u hunny~~

are you having fun at home w j

Marie Calloway
he just got home
marie was sleeping
i love u
dont sleep on the couch

ok i won't 😢

Marie Calloway
k
mew
i wanted us to be close
now seems impossible for me to feel uncomfortable since i got scared/sad
but i miss u
mew

"i feel alone in the world right now."
"i guess i always feel that way, but i don't really think about it."

he didn't come home until 4 A.M. i stayed up until 2 A.M. waiting for him. eventually i fell asleep, using his jacket as a blanket. i woke up to him looking down at me, smiling, while he stroked my hair. i felt like i wanted to be very kind to him from then. i felt very happy and warm. i wanted to be with him. i want to be his. i wanted to always be with him so he could always show me affection like that. i wanted him to always be stroking my hair.

i'm physically very beautiful, but my personality is terrible.

o........,.,.,..,.,.,
i don't think i like the internet

Marie Calloway
why

i just am not used to seeing someone rely on it so heavily for
relationships and things. i don't know i guess it is unsettling

Marie Calloway
k
idgi i was upfront about being a shy weirdo internet hermit before i came

i guess i just didn't know what that implied.
i'll see you tonight when i get off work

Marie Calloway
k

i need to clean things
miss you tons

*my life is stupid. it should be
ended immediately.*
"you don't have it in you to make
a work of art."
later i would apologize for saying
that to him.

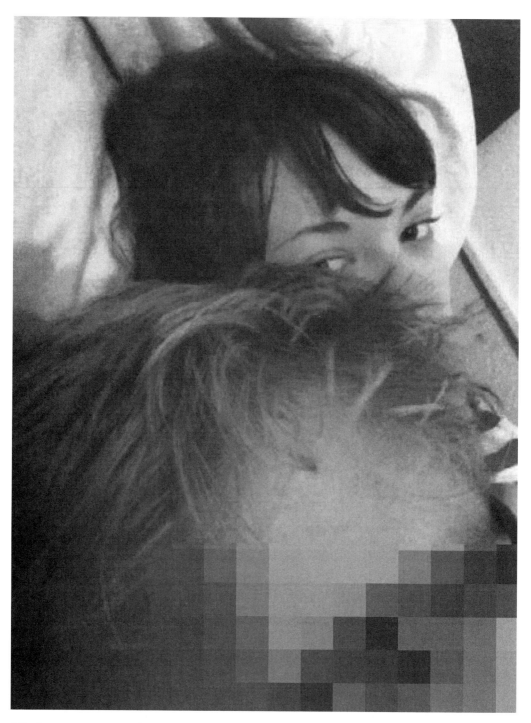

"i have mixed-feelings about you."
i like my life here.

Marie Calloway   Yesterday 🗩
i bought a bunch of snacks and etc to my bf at work
then i bought his roommate flowers
now im home
tired

                                                                       Yesterday 🗩
That is nice
Sounds like you are trying hard

 Marie Calloway   Yesterday 🗩
idk
we went to see a movie last night
im trying to be really nice
but its not really owrking out
sad
im going home friday morning tho

"We've already had this conversation."
There have always been many, many, many men who have fallen in love with the idea of Marie Calloway, and now that you're a micro-celeb it's only intensifying. When are you going to learn your lesson?

maybe you should stop jumping head over heels into relationships with strangers on the internet, especially ones who are all about your writing, and try crawling before you can walk

this is like the third or forth time this has happened since i've known you

not putting you down here i legit think maybe you should work on loving yourself and all that before thinking others will

stop telling me

Marie Calloway

thats true

im getting better kinda

this one i know i shouldn't have gone but i did

how stupid

i'll be able to keep myself from it next time hopefully since this was such a bad experience

i am. i already

you seem to keep getting into relationships for completely wrong reasons and hoping it'll fill soem void or whatever

then it turns out awful because either you aren't ready or the guy is a horrible douchebag

you simply aren't getting anything out of it

know.

Marie Calloway

true

"i could change my ticket easily so i don't leave on friday, but i guess you don't want me to."

"yeah, i guess i'd prefer it if you didn't change it."

"i don't think you're in love with me."

i hate it when other people try to tell you how you feel.

i began to sob.
he laughed at me. "It's okay. You're not in love with anyone!" "you've been very sweet and cute the past day or two. i feel like i'd be very attracted to you if i hadn't already seen a side of you i didn't like."
how could someone be so cruel

Marie Calloway
ill feel better when im home im sure
but
how oculd he be so mean
how could he dislike me so mych
he wont even touch me
not even care when im crying

Cos he's not. Nice boy

Marie Calloway
or want to be around me

He's a dick
That's it. Leave today

Marie Calloway
i guess it was obvious
for instance marie went out to socialize w her friend
and didnt come home til midnight
zac didnt stop playing cmputer game etc to sit with me or anything
im such a foool

he won't even touch me.
just say you hate me already. please be
honest. i'm not even worth that, to him.
"i'm not a doll." i'm not either.
all of that effort for nothing.
i guess i admire his life

working at american apparel and art movie theatre with many cool attractive hipster
friends and always going out and being v social and well liked
my life isn't like that at all
and i liked cuddling/sex/etc with him

how could he dislike me so much

Product	Cost
marie calloway's ticket	$10.00
One Way; 1 Adult: This fare is restricted to 1 adult and is refundable until 48 hours prior to outbound departure. From Ann Arbor (Blake Transit Center), MI to Detroit Metro Airport (North Terminal-Ground Transportation), MI Departing on 06/01/2012 07:45 AM, MFL 8006 w/ 1 bags	
Sales Tax	$0.00
Total Amount Paid	$10.00

MICHIGAN FLYER
BOARDING PASS   1141719A-1

FROM: ANN ARBOR (BLAKE TRANSIT   MI   DEP: 01Jun12 07:45am
        CENTER)

TO: DETROIT METRO AIRPORT   MI   SCHED MFL 8006
        (NORTH TERMINAL-GROUND
        TRANSPORTATION)

OW-1A ADULT   MARIE CALLOWAY

"[You're too sexually forward. It's very
unarousing."]

Marie Calloway

mew

idk

he has v high sex drive

but doesnt want to have sex w me much

i need a lot of sex/touching/etc to feel loved etc

Marie Calloway

he told me how he tried to cheat on his gf with his gf's friend before

it broke my heart to hear

idk

:<

ive never felt so sad/insecure with a guy

i know he only saw me as a concept; marie calloway the writer who is friends with tao lin and does readings in new york so nothing i could have done would have made him love me but it hurts very much not to be liked

What terrible things is he texting his friends about me?

zac acts sociopathic

but i guess it's just b/c he's so young and good looking people are treated better also which leads to sociopathicness idk

im glad i was ugly teenager so i didnt get the jerk attitude

yes feel the same

thank god for aspergers

"i feel like you don't want to be around me."
"that'sallthat i want to do today."
no, you want me to go home. please
stop pretending to like me to be polite. it's
humiliating.
"come out with me. don't sulk in my bed all
day, it's depressing."
"i'm sorry."
you have to understand. there's nothing
you can do that will make him comfort you,
not crying, not sleeping on the couch. you
mean nothing to him.
I'm sure he thinks I'm insane. But I'm not
insane!!

i'm tired; i tried.

i wish i were normal.
i wish i were normal.
i wish i were normal.
i wish i were normal.
i wish i were normal.
i wish i were normal.
i wish i were normal.
i wish i were normal.

i wish i were normal.
    "Please don't be mean after I leave."
           "I'm never mean!"
i feel very sad and alone in the world.
maybe i'm incapable of being loved like
this. how can i fix myself?
~fin~
p.s.:

Marie Calloway
i know u dont like me at all bur i miss being near u
it was very wonderful feeling when u touched me
feel chemically attached to u like i did the first time we talked
i know u will make fun of me/im humilating myself
wish i could be around u always
i dont care that you are mean and dont like me
i restricted u cos it will break my heart when i see tweets about u
sleeping w other girls and whatever
miss u terribly

never contact me again...

bdsm

"You are a very odd girl."

"How am I odd?"

"You don't look at me when I talk to you."

"Why do you enjoy being dominated?"

"I don't know."

"You've never thought about it? You don't ever write about your sexual experiences?"

"No," I said.

"Oh. I thought all writers did that. I do that," he said.

were the roughest. But a few days ago a guy made me throw up for real idk

Oct 8, 2012, 1:30 AM

Ha! I was looking forward to being the 1st to make you Really puke. And 75 is impressive. You're sucha whore. I love it. You gotta tell me more in person.

Where are you finding all these boys? And what constitutes "really" puking? Was tonight's flavor fun?

I don't know. Men like me.

Text Message Send

"Let's see how my hickey compares to this other fucking guy's."

*

He put his hand around my neck and applied some pressure. I couldn't moan like that and just breathed shallowly through my mouth. I glanced at him, and he was smiling. He applied more pressure and my breathing got shallower.

"You're not on birth control, are you?"

"No."

"Too bad. I wanted to creampie you."

I thought that was weird, that he would say 'creampie' instead of 'cum inside'. I guessed it was the influence of too much pornography.

*

"Say that you like being my piece of meat."

*

"Who was rougher?"

"You are."

"How am I rougher?"

"Because you hit me."

"I do hit you. And some just because I can. And you know why I can?"

"Because tonight you own me."

"That's right. That's what I want to hear. Say it again."

"You own me."

"I fucking love your voice. Such a girl…"

*

"Don't you ever fucking pull away when I'm fucking your throat, you understand that?"

"Yes."

"What do you understand?"

"That I won't pull away."

*

"Do you know how much that fucking turns me on, you struggling for air?"

*

"Do you want to be my pussy or my dog?"
"Your pussy."
"Meow for me."
I started to giggle.
"Come on. You say it over text."
I kept giggling, embarrassed.
He hit me repeatedly until I meowed.
"Come on. More. You need to convince me you're in heat."
…
"Meow with my cock in your mouth."
I did.
"Again."

*

"I want to be fucked."

*

"You're throwing up already?"

*

He wrote on my face with green marker.
"What does that say?"
I giggled a lot. "I can't read it…"
He hit me. "What do you think it says?"
I kept giggling, embarrassed.
He hit me again.
"It says 'whore'."

*

"Tell me that you're my whore."
"I'm your whore."
"I'm a piece of shit whore."
"Damn right you are."

*

I stared at myself in the mirror
"What?" he asked.

"My eyes are all red," I said. The whites of my eyes were completely red.

"I know."

*

"You're not being a good sub."

"I don't care."

"Did I awaken some hidden trauma?" he asked.

"No."

"You realize how aloof you're being?"

"Yes."

"What's like, the most brutal thing you did to a girl?"

"I've made a few girls throw up blood. I've made a few pussies bleed, too. And I made one girl puke and made her slurp it all up."

*

"My cock looks huge in your tiny mouth."

*

"has any guy ever cum on your face before?"
"yeah."

I don't feel degraded or aroused. I don't feel anything right now.

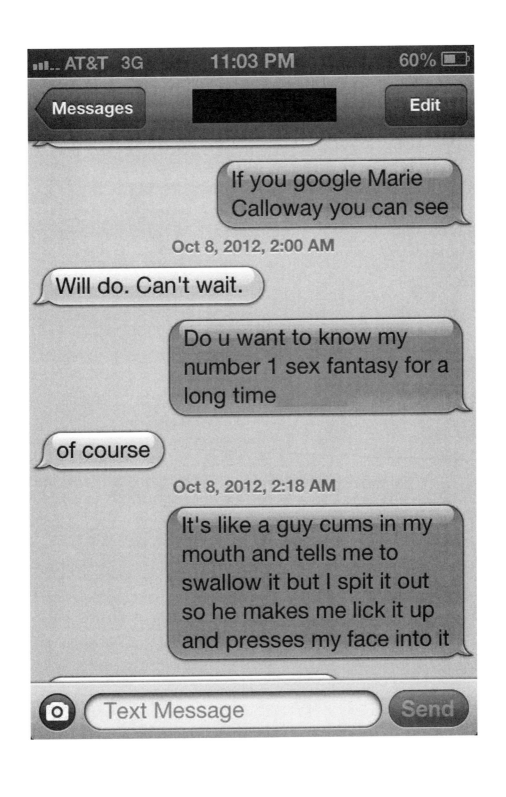

He emptied the condom into my mouth.

"Are you going to spit it out or swallow it?"

"You know what's coming now. Lick."

(Imagine what it tastes like to lick up cum emptied from a condom on top of a towel covered in vomit.)

"Again."

*

"Say nice things about me," I said.

"You're very cute. You have a cute voice. You dress well. And you're submissive like no other."

*

"come on, taste yourself."

he jammed his fingers down my throat.

"that's right, you fucking slut."

Those pictures are crazy.

Marie Calloway
how so

Oh come on

Marie Calloway
??

Full frontal pictures on FB...
and you're covered in bruises

Marie Calloway
lol

Did you get beat up... hardcore porn

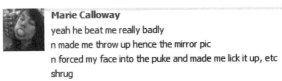

Marie Calloway
yeah he beat me really badly
n made me throw up hence the mirror pic
n forced my face into the puke and made me lick it up, etc
shrug

Pretty gross.
You like that?

Marie Calloway
yeah it was fun

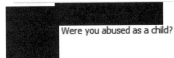

Were you abused as a child?

"Stop resisting and open your fucking mouth."

*

To look someone in the eyes is very hard for me, and he knew it.
I averted my gaze downwards.
He slapped me and yelled, "I said 'chin up!'"

*

Pectus excavatum

Hi Bunny its Dad
Are you ok I heard you vomiting
To be objectively beautiful you need to be a vessel
It were an objectively cold house I kept

*credit: bunny
rogers/cunny4.tumblr.com

"Come on bitch, I wanna fucking see you cry."

*

I gasped from the pain. I didn't know that being hit could hurt that badly.

*

"Open that fucking whore mouth."

*

I put my arms in front of my face, trying to protect myself from him.
"No, that's right. If you can't take it get on the fucking floor."
He grabbed me roughly by my hair and rubbed my face across a towel he had laid on the floor that was now covered in my vomit.

"Do you feel gross?"

I nodded.

"Do you like it?"

I nodded.

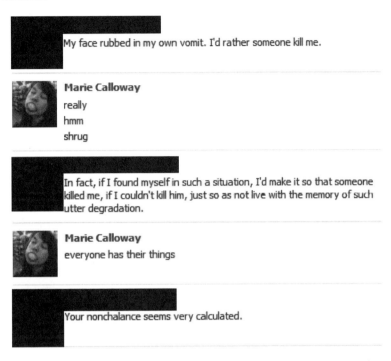

My face rubbed in my own vomit. I'd rather someone kill me.

Marie Calloway
really
hmm
shrug

In fact, if I found myself in such a situation, I'd make it so that someone killed me, if I couldn't kill him, just so as not live with the memory of such utter degradation.

Marie Calloway
everyone has their things

Your nonchalance seems very calculated.

*

"Shut the fuck up!"

it was the same tone, cadence as when i was little and my stepdad would yell at me. and i freezed up and became detached like i did when i was little. *frequently, girls/women who write about sex or have any sort of public creative life at all i would say are made fun of for having "daddy issues", and i was really scared of being assigned with that label so i shied away from discussing or even allowing myself to think about those things. but i realize this is really important to explore, kind of at the core of my whole project. and men are going to say these things anyway why should i give into it why should you let men control the conversation the conversation of yourself and your own sexuality. it's scary that being tarnished by a label can make you too afraid to even think about something.*

"Calm the fuck down!" he yelled and slapped me across the face. A week later, I was with my boyfriend and I was drunk and overly emotional. I thought then about how I wanted him to tell me to calm the fuck down and slap me, hard, like R had. *That's what I need from a boyfriend...*

Oct 20, 2012, 12:36 AM

Mew I want you to own me complete

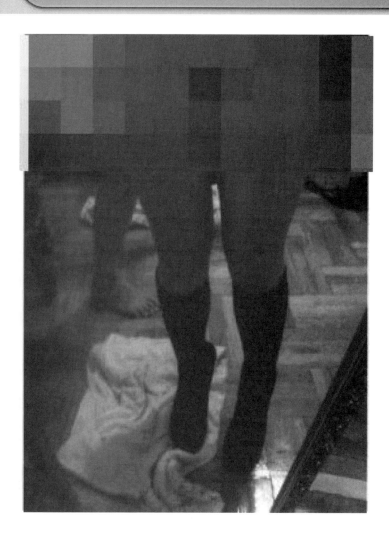

"This feels too good, this looks too good."

Marie Calloway

i have dad issue upon dad issue, like a wobbling jenga tower

Unlike · Comment · 4 hours ago near New York, NY · 🏛

Marie Calloway
not that i know of
i got annoyed w him before cos hes like pretentious etc
but i realized hes just really young n insecure and pretends to be older

And he likes to rub people's faces in their own vomit?

 Marie Calloway
yeah

How is vomiting--one of the more unpleasant physical sensations-
pleasurable?

 Marie Calloway
i guess its more like

 Marie Calloway
getting facefucked so hard that u vomit

 Marie Calloway
n it feels v intense
i just like
intensity etc cos u get to feel out of your head

Really, I've never felt that way hunched over a toilet bowl, sweating,
then choking the acidic contents of my gut.

The contrary: I've ll wished I could get out of myself: anywhere but
there.

.ıll. AT&T 3G   3:19 AM   70% 🔋

< Messages   [████████]   Edit

Facebook banned me for a day for posting those pictures

the bruised tit or were there more? And only a day?? Are they still up? You should send me my doing. my work of art on your body :-)

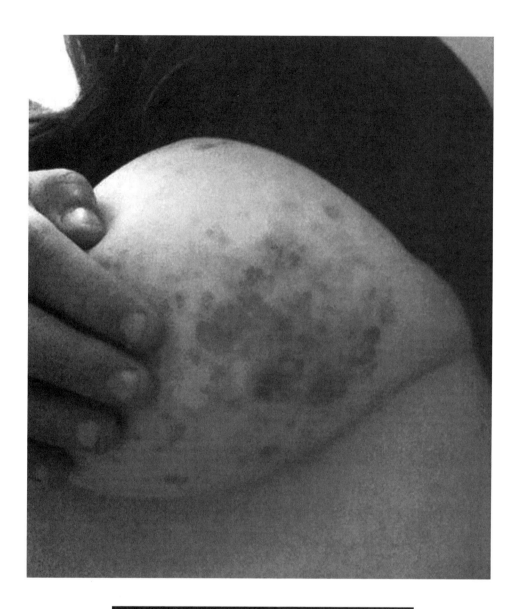

if this masochistic self-exploitation is third wave
feminism i don't like it.
3 hours ago · Like

you don't have to work towards liberation, but here
you're working in the service of oppression.

In a truly liberated society, I wonder if this class of perversion--related to domination and submission--would eventually go away.

?

I don't know if I like this. I must like it in a sense because I came back. It's more like I don't know if I'm enjoying it because I get off on this or if I'm just making myself act out past trauma and it's like a psychological issue thing... There's that same feeling of detachment is it okay because I get to feel out of my head... Is it detachment? I don't think it's a good thing to feel detached, or to make yourself feel that way...

*

"Say, 'I want your cock, Daddy.'"
"I want your cock, Daddy."

*

"Shut the fuck up!" he yelled and slapped me.

Later, I would tell my boyfriend to tell me to 'shut the fuck up' if he wanted to, as a favor to me.

*

"You took it pretty well. Do you feel proud that you can take so much brutality?"

"I feel neutral." *I feel like it would be a sad day when I start priding myself on that.*

*

"[I feel like there's such a limited way that you can be socially acceptable in this world]" my roommate, Lonely Christopher, told me after people complained to him about me.

19 minutes ago near Brooklyn, NY ·

My roommate Marie Calloway was temporarily banned from Facebook because some prudes misread her exploratory measures as provocation. Thanks a lot, you sick fucks.

"What did your Facebook friends say about those pictures?"

"Most people didn't like them…I got called a misogynist…"

"They called me a misogynist? Or you?"

"Me. For posting those pictures."

"But did you explain that it's not misogynistic because of Fuck Me Feminism?"

"People have different ideas about that sort of thing…"

"I understand that. It's very paradoxical… Do you think it's misogynistic?"

"I've never thought about it."

"I'm asking you to think about it now and tell me your opinion."

"I'm not intelligent enough to have an opinion."

*

marie: i understand if you don't respond to this msg, and i am sorry for emailing you, and i agree that my comment on your FB photo was not a good way to go about generating discourse.

however: i think that above all what i think you should know about the images you posted is that to some while they may seem like a positive affirmation of BDSM/'ruff' sex I think to others (like myself) they can also be triggering images that may imply sexual assault or rape.

that is all.

thank you for
touching me

*A*ugust 2, 2012
"I'm by the Lorimer stop at M Noodle. What are you doing?"

"I'm at a hotel in Manhattan."

"We're going to a gig then a hotel roof on Wythe. Let me know if you swing through the hood."

I didn't respond, and so Kip texted me again a few hours later.

"You still about? Thinking of heading."

"I'm around. You should come hang out."

"Is it cool if I come in a couple or so hours?"

"Okay."

Two hours later Kip texted me again.

"Yo badda bing, I'm dancing. I'm at an incredible gig with Chris Feldman, but he's tired and I'm full of energy. I'd like to come over later if you're feeling up for it—your last night dread da dread dread."

"Come! Bring Christopher."

"What's the hotel name and room number?"

"It's called Radisson. Room 1709. It's on 32nd st and Broadway."

"We're on the way x. Chris's much more lively now."

"Okay. I'm really tired by the way. Sorry if I'm half-asleep."

It was around 2 AM I had not slept in over 36 hours. I lay on the bed, trying to keep myself from falling asleep. I wondered how I would entertain Kip and Christopher with my exhausted zombie brain.

Kip and Christopher were two Facebook friends of mine in their early 20's from London. They happened to be in New York at the same time as I was visiting, and had asked me before to hang out while I was there. It was late at night then, and I had just wanted to go to sleep, but I thought that since Kip had been texting me throughout the week wanting to hang out that I should meet with him before I left, and tonight was my last night in New York.

Kip and I had talked about Scandinavia and Sheila Jeffreys and Jon Gnarr, ("I have a friend in New York who has been emailing back and forth with Jon Gnarr. Here's what he said to me, 'Do you think we should all move to Iceland? Speaking of comedians, I just got an email from Jon Gnarr saying he thinks Iceland could become an anarcho-socialist society but he needs all the good and creative people from around the world to come there and help…'")

Christopher had sent me long messages about literature and politics that I never bothered to read ("I'm writing my dissertation on contemporary experimental literature: is there an avant-garde today? What would being avant-garde today look like? Does that term even have meaning any more etc.… I read your thing on London and found it really interesting, especially as I can really imagine that sort of guy and see them around town a lot, and it's interesting reading about other people's experiences of London and as a guy it's obviously always interesting to hear about sex from the woman's point of view…").

*

About half an hour after his last text, Kip texted me that they were here, and a minute after that the room phone on the desk rang. I walked over to answer it.

"Miss, there are two people here who say they're here to see you."

"Okay."

I got up to go meet them outside, and we ran into each other at the entrance to the elevator. We said hello and laughed about almost missing each other. Kip and Christopher were lively and chatty in the elevator; I felt half-asleep and didn't say much.

I opened the door to my room and we all went in.

"This is *nice*. How did you afford it?" Kip asked.

"My friend, John, got it for us today, and then he went back home to Connecticut, so I have it for tonight."

We all sat on the edge of the bed.

"Can I have this?" I asked and picked up the beer Kip had set on the desk. He said it was fine, and I drank it rapidly.

"You're leaving tomorrow?" Christopher asked.

"Yeah, my flight's leaving at like seven in the morning," I said, laughing.

"Where are you going back to?" Christopher asked.

"The West Coast."

"So, you're not really Icelandic like you told me before? That's a shame… I wanted you to meet all of my friends in Reykjavik… I did my degree in Scandinavian studies," Kip said.

Christopher and Kip talked about going to Chicago. I talked about how rude people could be there.

"*Get the fuck out of my way!*" Kip said in an English accent-tinged imitation of a Chicago accent.

"London is full of cunts, too, though," Kip said.

"People in London can be like cold, I guess…" I said.

"Once late at night my friend was peeing on the street, and my friend was a girl, and a guy walked past and saw her and said, '*Not pretty, not classy!*' So that whole night we were all shouting 'not pretty, not classy!'"

"What have you been doing in New York?" Kip asked.

I started to laugh nervously. "I had a threesome with my friend and her husband, and it was one of the most awkward experiences of my life."

"But don't you think life is about those awkward moments and finding beauty in them…?"

I was too tired to formulate a response, so I just smiled.

"Are you one of those people who is really negative all of the time?" Kip asked.

"This guy who came over before you guys came—"

"*That's dread.*"

"What's 'dread'?"

"It's like over the top, extreme, in a good way."

"Anyway, the guy who came over before you guys came over was like, '*Oh baby,* I was really looking forward to coming over tonight.' And then I said, 'I look forward to dying.'"

Kip laughed and kissed me on the top of my head. I was surprised, but then I figured that it was just a natural expression of his extraversion.

"What's the best and the worst thing that's happened to you in New York?" Christopher asked.

"I threw up in my friend's bed."

"Was that the best or the worst thing?"

"It was kind of both."

Kip took out a bag of weed from his coat and asked me if I had any rolling papers; I didn't.

"Can you believe that we got all of this for twenty dollars?" Kip asked.

"The weed is a lot better here, right?" I asked.

"It might be better here, yeah…" Christopher demurred.

We decided to leave the hotel and walk down the street to Duane Reade to get rolling papers. Inside, Kip and Christopher picked out beer and bought it. At the counter, Kip asked for rolling papers, but the clerk said they didn't have any. He bought Parliament cigarettes instead, thinking that he could roll out the tobacco and use the paper.

Outside, we all smoked cigarettes on the street.

"I got you a present," Kip said and handed me an energy shot; he had shoplifted it.

"Oh, thank you."

Kip asked every passerby on the street if they had rolling papers. None did. I was interested in how he effortlessly, unselfconsciously engaged everyone, and charmed them. Christopher and I stood back, watching him. I drank the energy shot and made a face, but about fifteen minutes afterwards I felt much more awake.

"None of these people are the sort who would have rolling papers… We need to find a tramp," Kip said.

A disheveled looking man approached us and asked Kip for a cigarette. Kip gave him one.

"What kinda cigarettes are these?"

"These are Parliaments. You know, the crackhead cigarettes with the extended tip."

"Where are you from?"

"I'm from London."

"You sound like you's from London."

"Yes, I should hope so," Kip said.

"I heard ya'll call cigarettes 'fags' in London. Is that true?"

Kip confirmed that it was.

"*I'd like to bum a fag,*" Christopher said in an imitation of an American accent.

The man took the cigarette from Kip and walked away.

"I feel like the accent doesn't matter much in New York. Too cosmopolitan or something. *Don't they know who we are?*" Kip said.

"Yeah, how important we are…" Christopher added.

After a few more rejections, Kip said, "Let's give up." Christopher and I followed him back to my hotel room.

I sat down on the bed because I felt so tired. Kip sat down next to me and without hesitation pressed his body against mine and kissed me. I felt confused as I had gotten the feeling that he wasn't attracted to me. I had thought that the idea of anyone being attracted to me then, with my tired face without make-up, messy hair, and old, wrinkled clothes was unthinkable.

"Can I use your shower?" Kip asked.

"Go ahead."

Kip went into the bathroom and closed the door behind him.

Christopher sat down next to me on the bed.

"What ethnicity are you?" he asked.

"I'm part Korean and part German."

"I can see the German in you. Germans are always funny."

We talked about London and different places we had traveled to and how much we liked Japan.

I was slightly drunk, and liked the idea of making out with Christopher while Kip couldn't see us, so I moved to kiss Christopher.

"We don't have to kiss," he said, but I pressed and we began to make out.

Kip came fully dressed out of the bathroom and looked over at us. We stopped kissing and Christopher got up and went to sit in a chair across the room and went on his phone.

Kip sat down on the bed next to me. As I began to talk he kissed the top of my head and then he kissed me on my mouth. And then his hands were under my sweater and then reaching under my bra. He fondled my breasts and then unbuttoned my shirt and took off my bra. He kissed my breasts for a long time. I heard Christopher shuffling around the hotel, moving things around awkwardly. *Is he really doing this in front of his friend?* I couldn't tell if I was more uncomfortable or excited.

And then Kip's hand was under my skirt and he rubbed my clit through my underwear. I felt uneasy that Christopher was there and obviously felt very uncomfortable. I felt confused as to what was happening. *Are we really just going to have sex in front of his friend?*

Kip slid his fingers inside of my underwear and began to finger me. I moaned softly. I was amazed how unlike most guys he wasn't at all afraid or nervous. He wanted me and so he sat down next to me and started to kiss me and feel me up. He didn't care that his friend was there. Kip pulled my skirt down. I felt incredibly embarrassed to be almost naked and fingered in front of Christopher.

"Look at me," Kip said.

I looked into his eyes, which were bright green. He had a truly beautiful face. I blushed from the intensity, from being forced to realize he was looking at my tired, naked face from only a few inches away.

"Is this alright?" He asked.

I shut my eyes and nodded.

Kip got up and walked across the room to look in his bag.

I lay on the bed totally naked except for my underwear. I looked and saw Christopher now lying on the other side of the bed, looking at his iPhone.

"Chris, would you pull them down, please?" Kip asked. Christopher looked up from his phone. I wondered what was going to happen.

Christopher crawled across the bed and slid my underwear down.

Kip went down on me while Christopher kissed me and then my breasts. The feeling of having two men touch me at the same time was strange; it was pleasurable and interesting because it was a totally new sensation, but it was also overwhelming to the point that I sought to disassociate. And it was tainted by the worry that afterwards they would think less of me. It was interesting to me, the way that two men could, with their bodies, actively physically create a reason to respect me less, that they could transcribe shame onto my body with their own. Christopher put his fingers into my mouth.

Kip kissed me on the mouth and then my ears and neck and Christopher immediately went down on me.

I looked up and saw Kip handing an unwrapped condom to Christopher. This excited me; I felt like I was a present being given to Christopher by Kip.

Christopher put on the condom and penetrated me and lifted my legs high into the air. Kip made out with me. I struggled to kiss him because I kept moaning. He stuck his tongue so far down my throat that I gagged, which I liked.

"Look at me," Kip said.

I turned my head to look up at him, but didn't open my eyes.

"Very hot. Very sexy," he said forcefully.

I wondered if I seemed like I needed to be consoled about the way I looked… I was no longer really insecure about the way I looked. I felt incredibly embarrassed yet excited that I was being fucked while Kip watched, and on a deeper level I felt scared because of some more intimate fear, insecurity that I didn't understand that Kip and the situation in general tapped into. Perhaps I was just afraid of him.

Kip motioned to Christopher, and he immediately stopped fucking me. Kip put on a condom and then penetrated me. I moaned loudly. He was much rougher than Christopher had been. I felt embarrassed, knowing that now they had both seen me fuck two guys in a row. *Had they talked about how I had written about being a sex worker in London? Had they talked about how I write about sex? Had they thought I would be so easy and that they could do whatever they want because they know that I write about sex…?*

I turned my head to look at Christopher, and saw him looking at Kip's cock going in and out of me. He looked fixated yet dumbstruck. I wondered what it was like to be a straight male and to watch your friend penetrate another woman, to see his sexual performance and his cock. I wondered if he felt aroused, excited, disturbed…. I imagined asking him later about it over Facebook chat.

"Turn over," Kip said.

I rolled over onto my stomach and got onto my hands and knees. Kip took me from behind and Christopher came to stand in front of me. I realized that Kip had directed the scene so that I would give Christopher a blowjob while Kip took me from behind. It was interesting to me how Kip was controlling not only me, but the other male, and how he did it subtly, without any force.

I heard the sound of them pecking each other on the lips.

I wondered what they would say to each other about it later. I wondered if they would make fun of me after they left. I imagined them imitating the sounds of my moans to each other and laughing. Part of me wanted to cry. I felt like they saw me as, were using me like, a machine.

Whenever I allowed myself to be used so blatantly I could never reconcile my excitement and my curiosity, my desire to experience, with the feeling of being dehumanizied and uncared for.

Kip wanted to switch places with Christopher, and so they stopped and began to circle around me. I lay on the bed, half-curled up, panting. I could tell that I had a pained expression on my face, and I didn't try to hide it. Part of me wanted to cry, but it wasn't overwhelming and so I could ignore the desire to. Christopher looked at me and then he said to Kip, "Do you want to take a break? We can all spoon or something."

Kip nodded and went to go sit on the floor and began to roll a joint. Christopher lay on the bed.

I felt an impulse to write, partly because I was upset and overwhelmed with feelings. Wordlessly, I walked over to the desk across the room and on the provided hotel notepad wrote in a stream-of-consciousness,

"*I felt like they were having sex with each other through me. The handing condoms & asking the lube, the desire to eat me out immediately after the other one had, and of course the desire to pass me around... Two penises in the same vagina as close as touching as could be allowed. Homosociality. English accents. The kiss during.*"

I tore the paper I had written off from the notepad and walked over to put it into my purse.

"Marie, are you okay?" Christopher asked.

"Yeah."

"Are you really okay?"

I nodded.

*

Kip finished rolling a joint, and we all went still naked into the bathroom to smoke it. Christopher stuffed a towel under the door so the smoke wouldn't get into the room.

"Do you guys say 'hotbox'?" Kip asked.

"I think that's just called putting a towel under the door," I shrugged.

Kip and Christopher conversed. I looked at myself in the mirror.

"Your areolas would be lighter if you were Icelandic," Kip said suddenly to me.

I blushed.

We all passed the joint around until it was gone.

"Can I smoke another one?" Kip asked.

"It's getting really smoky... There's like a two hundred dollar fine if they find out you smoked in the room..." I said.

"I don't know. I've smoked in a lot of hotels and it's never been an issue," Kip said.

"It's your room, though," Christopher said.

"Is it okay?" Kip asked.

"I'd prefer it if you didn't…." I said while nervously smiling.

Christopher opened the door to the room and Kip and I followed after I washed the ashes down the sink.

*

"It's almost 5 AM" Christopher said, implying that he and Kip would have to leave soon.

But I didn't want them to go. I wanted him to finish what he started; I wanted him to cum in me or on me. And I wanted to see what would happen if we kept going with this. It felt like something that I had to experience. I wondered if I was being driven by a self-destructive impulse.

I looked at Kip. He kissed me and we made out for a while. I tried to very gently pull him towards the bed. He pushed me onto the bed and violently pulled my shirt over my head and tugged my skirt down.

Kip kissed me deeply and began to finger me.

I wondered if men ever considered how having long nails makes fingering painful for girls. I thought about how with most men I would tell them to stop because it hurt, but with Kip…

"You sound so fucking sexy when you moan."

"Does that feel nice?" Kip asked.

"*Yeah…*"

He asked me repeatedly if it felt nice, even though I was moaning loudly and had responded affirmatively three times. I used to hate it when men got off mainly by getting women off; something felt humiliating and dishonest about it. But I had changed my way of thinking recently to enjoy the humiliation and control of being used in that way, though afterwards it left me feeling extremely used. I had actively adjusted my sexuality so that it was more compatible with a common male sexual urge. I was overwhelmed with embarrassment and shame and excitement.

Sometimes I would open my eyes and look up at him and see him looking directly back down at me, grinning.

"You like getting girls off?" I asked.

"Yeah, I love it."

"You know what would really get me off? If you were mean to me."

"Mean? I'll be a fucking cunt."

He bit me on my neck, thighs, arms, and breasts so hard that I yelped every time, that I still had red bite marks on my skin days later.

"*Fuck me…Fuck me…Fuck me…*" I moaned. I wanted to excite Kip, to push him in order to see all that he would do to me. I felt like there was something that I was seeking from this situation that I hadn't experienced yet.

"Chris, would you fuck Marie, please?" Kip asked.

I wondered why Kip wouldn't fuck me.

Christopher looked up from his phone and came over to the bed. He jacked off violently, trying to get an erection. "*Fuck me,*" I moaned again. Christopher was able to get an erection and penetrated me from behind. Christopher slapped me hard on the ass. I wondered if because he was in front of another straight male he felt the need to act more dominating than he normally would, or if because Kip had obviously controlled and dominated him in a sense that Christopher felt the need to assert power over me.

I turned my head backwards to look at Christopher. His eyes were only slightly open, and he was smiling.

"Do you like it?" I asked.

"It feels really good," he moaned.

We had sex for a few more minutes, and then Christopher stopped so that Kip could fuck me.

Kip softly pressed a spot on my back in such a way that I fell flat onto the bed, and then he turned me onto my back. He penetrated me and then slapped me across the face. I moaned loudly in response.

"Do you like it?" I asked.

"You have a hot cunt," Kip said.

I had never been fucked so deeply in my life. I covered my mouth with both of my hands to stop from screaming out, and also to provoke some sort of control from Kip. Christopher grabbed my arms roughly and pulled them down so that I couldn't help but scream out loudly. *I kind of feel like I'm being gang raped right now.*

It was like he never tired. Kip alternated between fucking me, fingering me, and going down on me and he did it all with incredible energy, even long into it. Finally I had to say, "Stop doing that. Stop," and smack Kip's hand away until he finally stopped and sat down next to me.

I feel Fucked To Death. Laying there I thought about a dream I had the night before where I had been criticized by people for writing a story with a scene that was meant to excite the reader by describing my sexualized murder. I thought about how my friend had texted me about how she wanted to sunbathe on a giant, ancient sea turtle. I thought about how I had drunkenly curled up half-asleep in my friend's lap a few nights ago at a party and how he had stroked my hair and said, "Oh Marie, what are we going to do with you?"

"Have you done that before?" I asked.

"Not with two boys," Christopher said.

"Not with Chris," Kip said.

"You've done it with another guy before? With two girls is fun, too…"

Kip decided that we should all share a cab, they would drop me off at the subway station and then take it back to Brooklyn where they were staying.

*

Kip and I stood outside of the hotel while Christopher stood in the street, waiting to hail a cab. Kip hugged me and kissed me on the head and then my cheek. I felt upset and irritated. I didn't want him to be affectionate towards me, to pretend to feel any sort of emotion towards me. I didn't understand how I felt about Kip then. I thought about those people for whom it seems like other people don't really exist, but also how I had been complicit and even active in Kip acting out his self-image. I thought about how I had been full of desire to believe that he was more special than others in the hopes of him involving me in some sort of transcendent experience. I wondered if we had used each other for different (masculine/active; feminine/passive) roles in the same fantasy. And Christopher was in some strange place in between… I thought about how I would be left with all of these strange emotions while Kip wouldn't think of me at all.

"I hope that was okay," Kip said.

"How do you mean?" I felt like acting coy. Or, I didn't want to concede that what had happened hadn't upset me.

"I hope it was more fun than awkward and weird."

"Was it for you?"

"For me, definitely."

He asked me where I was from.

"I'm from Portland."

"A lot of lovely things come from there. You have a lot to live up to."

"I don't want to live up to anything. Like, I don't know…"

We talked a little more, and then Christopher finally stopped a cab. We all got in. I sat in the middle. Kip lay his head on my shoulders, and I leaned against Christopher. I wondered when I would stop abusing myself for the sake of new experiences, new sensations. No one talked during the cab ride.

When it arrived at the train station we all got out. Kip said that it had been lovely to meet me, and hugged and kissed me. Christopher hugged and kissed me and said, "Have a lovely trip back to wherever it is you are going."

Marie Calloway (b. 1990) is a writer and resident of Manhattan.